The Dream Catcher Tour

Keep in touch with your dreams - always!

Enjoy —

Paula Buermele

Paula Buermele

Outskirts Press, Inc.
Denver, Colorado

Outskirts Press
Denver, Colorado
http://www.outskirtspress.com

ISBN-10: 1-4327-0353-6
ISBN-13: 978-1-4327-0353-0

Library of Congress Control Number: 2007920971

Outskirts Press and the "OP" logo are trademarks belonging to
Outskirts Press, Inc.

Printed in the United States of America

Women On Board

"Go back. They can't take a party of forty-seven," directed Madeline. The women began their retreat, simultaneously turning around in the narrow aisle of the supper club. Two by two they filed back to the tour bus, disappointed that the tantalizing aroma of steak and seafood would quickly be replaced by diesel fumes.

Emily slipped her professional smile into place and reassured the ladies that they would see a "Buses Welcome" sign soon. Nightfall came late this far north in midsummer, so she was not concerned about whether they had time to find another restaurant and still arrive at the hotel before the driver need concern himself with deer in the headlights.

Northern Experience Tours promoted economical, no-frills excursions around the Great Lakes. The emphasis was on cleanliness, comfort and relaxation, which appealed to a band of travelers who wanted to add a new layer of life experience while managing on a limited budget. The adventurousness of the experience depended heavily on the tour guide and the availability of little-advertised events in the various towns on their itinerary.

This particular tour happened to include only women; forty-seven women, to be exact. They were the kind of women who had not yet disengaged from their interest in life or their environment; they had embraced relationships past and present and did not discount forming new ones in the future. Of course, this knowledge was not evident from their registration forms—it was what Emily had observed over the first few days after their departure from Chicago.

A quick, last look over her shoulder confirmed that her charges were settled once more in their coach seats. They reminded her of eggs sorted neatly in a carton: premium grade A, size large. Her curiosity was piqued as she wondered what lay beneath their polished shells. Her own superficial imperfections were cleverly camouflaged beneath expensive makeup and measured style. What blemishes and minor cracks would become visible on her companions as they traveled together?

Twenty years ago Emily's career path had not included tour guide responsibilities. Career paths are notorious for taking odd twists and turns, and even for petering out altogether. But whether it was a career path or a cart path, some path had to pay the bills, and Emily found her work with Northern Experience Tours to be an adequate road for her current needs.

Pulling the soft sweater around her slender shoulders, she gazed out the window as the Lake Michigan shoreline came into view. The ladies had agreed to wait for one more hour for their dinner and travel on to Manistique, their destination for the night. The Kewadin Casino Night was eagerly anticipated by the ladies and now that Emily had a multitude of trips in her experience arsenal, she knew that watchfulness was all that would be required of her. She also knew the food would be fabulous and no dinner reservations were required.

Charmed by the evening shadows that stole over the ragged beach as it passed by her window, Emily slipped into a warm pocket of memory and thought about one pleasant path she had explored too briefly not long ago.

A Fish Tale

Emily settled into the wicker chair on the back porch of the small cabin, flipping open the cover of her laptop as she adjusted the cushions behind her. Listening to the soft sound of the trees swaying overhead, she vaguely noted that the Whispering Pines Motel was aptly named. A refreshing breeze, the moon reflecting its pale path across the bay, and the chirp of crickets nearby stirred her memories of childhood summer days spent with her grandparents in this lovely area. No time for reminiscing now, she thought, as she clicked on the e-mail from her friend, Anne.

Emily, I am so glad you were able to take vacation time to come and help me with the art exhibit opening in two weeks. I am so new to this job, and Escanaba is nothing like Ann Arbor, so finding the right tone for the gala has been tricky. I look forward to seeing you tomorrow—and discussing these mysterious messages from Eric. Anne.

Emily looked forward to seeing her friend, too. They had been roommates at the University of Michigan and had kept in touch over the years as each pursued separate career paths. Emily had taken her liberal arts degree to Chicago and settled there, while Anne had remained in Michigan developing her interest in art and going on to manage art galleries.

After hitting the 'sleep' button on her computer, Emily set it aside and picked up *The Daily Press*. Flipping through the pages, she looked for the personal ad that contained the message Anne had mentioned. She needed to help her friend solve this little mystery.

Dir A from AA: Three has the key. Remind you of someone?

She knew the ads referred to her friend, but neither she nor Anne knew what they meant or why they were being placed. That would be the first thing they discussed tomorrow morning.

"Now, tell me everything," Emily said as they settled into a booth at the 8th Street Coffee House. "How do you know that these ads are meant to get your attention?"

"It started with our newest exhibit at the gallery. We wanted to show a collection of art with fresh water fish as the theme. We sent invitations to local artists a year ago and started getting acceptances last winter. One artist, Eric, submitted a request to show a series of five paintings. His sketches showed walleyes, captured in oil, and they had a captivating sense about them, a vibrant character. The panel immediately accepted them and I was assigned to inform him, validate his qualifications for the exhibit, and get general information about him."

"What did you find out?"

"Nothing much, just that he had been raised in the Upper Peninsula and eventually returned and set up residence in the area again. Residency is all he really needs." Anne moved her tea cup aside to make room for the huge cinnamon roll placed before her.

Emily took a bite out of her blueberry muffin and raised her eyebrows at the treat in front of her friend. She didn't say anything about the roll but recognized it as a sign that her friend was far more nervous than she was willing to admit.

"Go on, Anne, what raised your suspicions?"

"Well, when I interviewed Eric he seemed very reluctant to answer any questions about his background or talk about his work. I certainly have met a lot of artists through my work and he was unlike any of the others—almost hostile. He refused to give me any information for the exhibit identification signs that will be posted by his work. When the first painting arrived, there was a note to *Dir A of AA* that said to look for a clue in each painting to answer the question in the paper. I only spoke to him on the phone so I don't know what he looks like, nor can I even guess his age."

"Tell me about the paintings," Emily urged as she held out her coffee cup for a refill of the flavor of the day: Mackinac Island Fudge.

"The first one shows a single, huge walleye against an abstract background of deep blue and yellow. It's got a huge mouth, which is wide open. I searched the paper that night and found a personal ad that said *Dir A of AA: Look familiar?* The second painting has two large walleyes swimming against a golden, abstract background. This time the fish are chasing smaller ones. These fish look downright ferocious. The second ad warned that *its nature's course, you can't hide*."

"And the third painting...?"

"This time the walleye is diving down to the bottom, again with its mouth wide open. I see now that the difference between his series and the other art we've received for the collection is that the fish in his works have these huge, wide open mouths and the others show the fish with closed mouths."

"Are you sure you don't know this guy from somewhere? You spent a lot of time working with various artists' groups when you were in Ann Arbor."

"I worked more with fundraisers and organizers and the business side of art than with the artists themselves. I have sat on a lot of art juries but I think I would have recognized his style if I had seen it before. I just don't know what to make of this unusual mode of communication."

They walked into the cool breeze coming off Little Bay de Noc and headed to the art center two blocks away. The art gallery and gift shop had just opened its doors for the day and Emily impulsively pulled her friend inside.

"I want to look around a little. I can meet you at the art center if you want to get to work right away," Emily said as they entered.

"No, I'll look around, too. Mallory is a new friend of mine and a good source of information about the local artists. I'll see what she knows about Eric," Anne replied.

Emily hovered near the jewelry art and admired the copper-hammered rings as she listened to Anne and Mallory's conversation.

"No, I've never met Eric," Mallory replied, "but I have seen his work at various exhibits. His oils sell pretty well, I understand. I know he grew up around here but then left, as most young people do." She then turned to Emily and offered to answer any questions about the jewelry she was admiring. Emily was very interested in having a ring on her finger, but not one that she had to put there herself.

They left the store and reached the William Bonifas Fine Arts Center. "This is beautiful!" Emily exclaimed as she looked at a handsome Romanesque structure of golden Kasota stone.

"The exterior has been maintained in its original state since it was built in 1938. But the interior has been remodeled and is totally modern. It even includes a theater. Come inside."

Anne hung her sweater over the back of her office chair and led Emily to the classroom area, where she showed her the gallery being set up for the fish art exhibit. Sculptures, bowls with fish motifs, and fish creel basket art were cleverly displayed on blocks in the center of the gallery, while paintings, fabric wall hangings, and even a quilt had been hung strategically on the walls. A bank of lights allowed individual focus on each object. They walked past the stairway leading to the upper gallery and into the workroom. The latest delivery was propped against the huge work table in the center of the room.

"It looks like number four has arrived," Anne stated, tucking her long brown hair behind her ear.

Emily helped her remove the brown paper wrapping and set aside the cardboard reinforcements. She studied the school of fish and admired the rich blend of colors that again suggested an underwater world. The image changed depending on how the light struck it, just as it would with real sunlight reflecting off a lake's surface. The walleye, its mouth wide open, was in the act of swallowing a smaller fish.

"Are you sure you aren't imagining this sinister effect?" Emily asked. "I'm just not seeing it."

"I'd agree with you if it weren't for the ads in the paper that follow each delivery. What does this guy want?"

"Are you scared?"

"No, I'm more creeped out than anything. Why does he want my attention?"

"Perhaps you will find out at the gala—he is attending, isn't he?" asked Emily.

"I doubt it, based on my conversation with him. However, in this region the gala is the best opportunity for selling his work, so I think it would be in his best interest to show up."

That night the message in the paper simply read *Dir A of AA: Number four, one more. Figured it out yet?*

A week later, the last painting arrived amidst the confusion of caterers coming and going to set up the tables and decorate for the opening of the exhibit the following night. The custodian carefully hung the final painting and adjusted the spotlight to catch the highlights in the murky, abstract lake bed. The walleye was camouflaged against a piece of sunken driftwood, its mouth open and lip curled around a tail fin.

Emily stood in front of the mirror in the motel cabin and twitched into place the black silk skirt covering the wide pant legs. Her velvet tube top, with its tiny emerald rhinestone trim, showed off her evenly tanned shoulders. The reflection also showed the knotty pine-paneled walls behind her and a low bookcase filled with Zane Grey dime novels and a variety of chick-lit volumes. A small lamp illuminated the cut-out figures of moose on its base. Talk about being a fish out of water, she thought. At least I don't look like a bridesmaid with an upswept hairdo, she observed as she brushed the long blonde locks down her slender back.

The plans she and Anne had arrived at for the gala included the Bay Jazz Band, and she could hear them warming up as she parked her car in front of the building. She hoped all would go well for her friend's debut as exhibit hostess and that they had chosen the right blend of sophistication and local culture for an enjoyable evening.

Scanning the room looking for her friend, Emily noted the beautiful floral displays discreetly placed along the walls, mimicking a shoreline. Going for a slightly campy effect, they had asked the wait staff to dress as fishermen, so the bartender was standing behind the bar in his hip boots and the attendants were dressed in flannel shirts and jeans. A mobile crafted from fishing gear hung airily above the buffet table.

"Emily," exclaimed Anne as she strolled towards her. "I want you to meet one of our patrons, Mrs. Parquette. She knows many of our featured artists."

"Please, call me Faith," Mrs. Parquette said. She looked to be a matron as much as a patron, with her stout figure draped in a flowing evening caftan. "Yes, I do know them because I taught many of them during my tenure at the high school. I make it a point to keep track of the better ones and encourage them to bring their talent back home. Why, there's Eric now—let me introduce you."

The women turned to see a tall, muscular man in his early thirties standing near a vase of cattails. He was dressed in blue jeans and a turtleneck under a brown corduroy jacket. The eyes raised to theirs were as cool and gray as the lake itself.

"Hello, Mrs. P," he said, nodding politely. "How's Mr. P?"

"He's fine, I'm sure, but I had to all but drag him here tonight. You know how he is about social functions. This is our hostess Anne, and her friend, Emily. Please excuse me. I must go rescue my poor husband from Sister Agnes before I have damage control to consider."

Eric did not smile as he gave his attention to the women. He looked at Anne.

"Did you get my messages?"

Anne was still trying to take in his physical appearance. Somehow, she had imagined a much older man, a character more in keeping with his gruff manner—certainly not someone so stunning.

"Yes, but I'll be honest—I haven't any idea what you are trying to tell me," she replied. "I think your work is outstanding, but I can't discern any special meaning to the messages. Please explain." She took a small step closer to Emily.

His sudden smile was echoed in his eyes. "Oh, it's not particularly deep. I just thought it was a subtle way to remind you of your previous judgment of my work. I entered a painting in a show ten years ago and you were on the jury. Your explanation for the rejection of my work included comments such as shallow, no depth, no action, amateur effort. I was furious at the time but I think I've grown some since then. When you called me to inform me of my work's acceptance, I knew you hadn't recognized my name. I couldn't resist the opportunity to tweak you a little."

Anne didn't know whether to be angry or to laugh at the clever payback.

"I too have grown in the past decade and I hope my critique style is far more polished now," Anne replied. She glanced at Emily and saw the look of fascination on her face. It was returned by Eric. Apparently, this story is just beginning, she thought, as she mumbled a soft general reply and deftly blended into a group nearby. They didn't miss her.

"So, you think my friend has a big, wide open mouth, huh?" Emily inquired, smiling.

*

Emily tuned back into the present and became aware of the two women sitting behind her. There were few private conversations on a tour bus and all participants knew that. Emily enjoyed listening to the stories the women shared. She often reflected on their experiences as she examined her own troubled transition to a new phase in her life.

11

Soccer Mom

J ean lowered the back of her seat to a more comfortable
incline. Reaching into her beaded tote, she pulled out a
snack-size plastic bag containing twelve unsalted
almonds. She was much more health conscious these days
and had learned a lot about nutrition through her experience
in caring for her mother-in-law. While she preferred the
taste of cheese puffs, the almonds would take the edge off
her hunger while providing some benefit to her heart.

Betty, her seat partner for this part of the trip, glanced
at the nuts. "Good choice," she commented as she shifted to
better accommodate her large frame in the seat. "I think I'll
try some of your snack ideas the next time we have an
opportunity to shop."

"My list of approved snacks has grown from the many
hours spent in various waiting rooms while my mother-in-
law is being treated," Jean responded. "It's a very different
list from the ones I packed while hauling my children from
one practice to another. I think the foods on that list
contributed at least twenty of the pounds I've worked so
hard to lose these past two years."

"How many children do you have?" asked Betty.

"Three daughters—the youngest left the nest a year

ago. My eldest is married and has a young child, the middle one has a good start on a solid career, and the youngest has settled into her college studies," Jean explained.

Smiling, Betty replied, "I suppose those practices you mentioned mean your daughters are all lovely and dance and sing and are accomplished musicians."

Jean laughed. "Well, I think they are lovely, but not as refined as you imagine. My husband wanted boys and while he waited in vain for a son to appear, he lost no time passing along his love for sports to his girls. Dale is a high school coach of both boys and girls. I've spent a good deal of my life sitting on bleachers and benches."

Jean leaned back and closed her eyes. Her daughters were indeed lovely. They had worked hard—and worked together—to surprise her with this trip as her Mother's Day gift. "It's your turn to be driven, Miss Daisy," they had told her. Not only had they raised the money to pay for it, they had worked out a care schedule to ensure that their grandmother didn't miss an appointment or any of her daily medications.

*

Before the leaves fell from the trees in the coming fall, Grandma Shirley would have to give up her tightly held independence. The last incident had convinced Dale and his brother that it was time.

"Dale, I walked in there and she had the table set for six people and was cooking up a storm. She asked me if Henri was in the garage—Henri's been dead for ten years, Dale. I thought I had convinced her that Henri wasn't coming in, ever, but she simply responded by getting out the Tupperware and saving him some food for when he came home."

"I know it's been really hard on you, dear, and both

13

Glen and I are very grateful that you take such good care of her. I do see that it's getting dangerous for her to be alone and the doctor has told us all that her Alzheimer's is reaching advanced stages. Glen and I will start looking for a care facility for her." Pulling his cell phone out of his pocket and flipping it open, Dale walked away, once more avoiding a deeper discussion about his mother.

*

Betty interrupted Jean's reverie. "I was just thinking that in our generation, there were no sports practices for girls. I recall the sports section in my year book featured all-boy sports while the girls were allowed intramural sports only. We never played anyone from any other school and certainly didn't have an organized practice outside of phys ed class."

"You're right, Betty," Jean replied. "We had three paths: Future Teachers, Future Nurses, and Future Homemakers. Title IX didn't come along until a couple of years later."

"Do you think your daughters learned the same toughness from their sports activities that we did from our restrictive role push? I know I resisted it," Betty smiled.

What an interesting observation, Jean thought. What had given her the strength she had needed to withstand the weathering of life? Was it just the school of hard knocks or the relationships built and broken over the years? What gave her the strength now?

She did know that this vacation was renewing her strength. She hadn't realized how much of her reserve had been consumed over the last couple of years.

Jean turned to her companion. "I think their sports

experience taught them the value of teamwork and now they find a family strength in that. Perhaps they are just maturing, but I never imagined that three such different personalities would actually successfully cooperate to give me this vacation and take on my responsibilities while I'm gone." Of course, she didn't know how successful they actually were in this commitment, given that she had promised that she would not call home at any time during her tour.

The bus pulled into the rest area. Betty left to stretch her short legs. Jean wondered how many times it had been she in the driver's seat, with a van full of soccer equipment and girls bickering over who had said what about whom. She didn't miss those trips! She did miss the quiet conversations with her daughters, however, on the trips where it was just the family. Somehow, the darkness on the ride home from an exhausting game blended the lines between mother and daughters and they were able to take their discussions to more intimate levels. Perhaps that was where their strength was nurtured.

Betty returned and settled into her seat. "All those trees out there reminded me that I was once a tomboy," she told Jean. "My escape was climbing the highest tree I could find. It was especially satisfying when the neighbor boys saw me and threatened to tell my mom. They were too afraid to climb that high," Betty confided. "I didn't outgrow that until I was fifteen. A girl I knew at school still climbed trees, but she fell out and was paralyzed from the waist down for the rest of her life. Seeing April in a wheelchair was enough to convince me—I never climbed a tree again."

Strength can be built in many ways, Jean reflected. It may come from building a skill or perhaps in meeting a challenge when some ability is taken away. Weaknesses were not always overcome, she knew, and sometimes failure killed the desire to try again. She hoped she would never be tested beyond her desire to keep her heart in whatever challenge she was given.

The bus pulled into the brightly lit parking lot and the women headed for the restaurant while Emily checked in at the front desk. After confirming their room reservations for the next two nights and signing the credit slip, she joined her group, which was now comfortably seated at several tables in a spacious dining room.

"We saved a place for you, Emily," Janice waved from a table near the fireplace. Emily still found the friendly acceptance of these women a little startling. Her long tenure in the business world had taught her to wrap her emotions in multiple layers of protectiveness. Trust resided in a back corner of her heart and was not easily teased out.

Emily took a quick glance at the menu but she knew that whitefish would be her choice tonight. Apparently, she still had fish on her mind.

"Look! A birthday celebration," Janice exclaimed as the wait staff gathered around a family tucked in the alcove near the window. "Wow! There are a ton of candles on that cake." The women shuffled their chairs to get a better look at the birthday girl. She was no girl—her frail frame and rounded back indicated a body that had survived many decades. But her alert expression and gentle smile suggested an appreciation of the attention she was receiving.

"I hope I age that gracefully," Emily remarked. She feared aging far more than she was ready to admit, to herself or anyone else.

"I hope that I am that well-loved when I am old," said Janice. "Oh, and I hope I do get that old."

"Aging is what you make it," Madeline announced.

Several chemically-enhanced heads of hair nodded in agreement. "And it's not about wearing purple or red, either."

"Remember how eagerly we anticipated our birthdays when we were kids?" Margaret asked. "I love the birthday rituals. What kind of traditions did everyone here celebrate?" Her question brought quick laughter and the stories began to flow as dinner was served.

Later that night, Ruth relived her favorite birthday, nearly fifty years ago.

A Golden Birthday

H er eighth birthday dawned bright, white and cold. The first good thing: it was Saturday, a day that always held the potential for surprises. Surprises of unanticipated happenings, some memorable, some not, all folded into the routine of the day. What surprises would this day hold?

She already knew it would not include a party, or more than one present. Dad was in the hospital, the victim of a drunk driver. Mom was struggling to keep her four young children fed and cared for without the benefit of Dad's paycheck or any insurance money. She did not drive, so managing visits to Dad was dependent on the charity of friends and neighbors.

The first surprise came at breakfast. Her mother handed her a package from her grandmother.

"Grandma sent a present in the mail?" she questioned excitedly. She couldn't believe it. Grandma had never sent an open-up present before. Usually it was just a card with two crisp dollar bills.

"Open it, open it," her sisters urged. They, too, were consumed with curiosity, and eager to see what it contained. The brown paper fell away to reveal a white, vinyl purse—a purse that blossomed with the fragrance of spearmint. It was crammed full with packs of her favorite gum. Just opening it caused the abundant contents to spill out—plenty to share with her siblings, and more than enough for her. What a treat!

The next surprise appeared when Mother walked into the room during the Saturday morning cartoons.

"Ruth, Mr. Newman is taking me to the hospital to visit Dad. Would you like to ride along? You will have to wait in the lobby for me—you know the hospital does not allow children to visit patients. I think you are old enough to wait alone in the lobby, don't you?"

Ruthie was thrilled. Her secret birthday wish had been to see her Dad, and while this chance didn't completely satisfy that wish, it was something. It also had the appeal of doing something without her older brother and two younger sisters.

Ruthie had been to the hospital many times with her Dad while tagging along on his milk route runs. She had only seen the dock area and the back of the kitchens. Nuns scared her, so she would fade into shadowy corners to observe them while Dad unloaded the milk crates. Her friends, who went to Catholic school, had informed her the nuns were mean so she did her best to avoid attracting their attention.

Today, though, she entered the front door of the hospital with her mother. Wrinkling her nose at the pungent medicinal odor, she promised mother she would not leave the lobby area and quickly found a seat where she could watch the busy activity. Nuns were scurrying here and there and every few minutes the chime of the elevator signaled another load of people to let in and out. The freight elevator was particularly interesting, as all manner of people and equipment came out of that door. As she absorbed the sights, sounds and smells of this special environment, she thought about her Dad and wondered what it was like on those floors above her head.

She unbuttoned her dark green sweater and settled back to count the packs of gum in her new purse and see if she could multiply five sticks per pack and get the correct answer. Then the freight elevator caught her attention again. She looked up to see a nun wheeling out a stretcher. The person on the stretcher, covered from head to toe with a white flannel sheet, was unmoving. Ruthie knew the morgue was in the basement so she quickly concluded that the patient must be dead or the face would not have been covered. But why had the elevator stopped on the main floor? Why was the nun wheeling a dead person around in front of everyone, especially a child?

Her amazement grew when the nun aimed the stretcher for the lobby and started rolling it towards her. The nun parked it expertly in the corner. The third surprise of the day had arrived: her Dad pulled the sheet off his face, sat up and said, "Happy Birthday, Ruthie!"

She ran into his arms and buried her head in his shoulder, hardly daring to believe her own senses. He had grown a beard and looked much thinner than she remembered. His right hand was wrapped in a huge bandage. Dressed in his robe, with a narrow bandage wound around his head, and his new beard, he reminded Ruthie of a disciple from her children's Bible. His smile and sparkling eyes quickly convinced her she wasn't dreaming—it was really her father. They quietly cuddled together on the couch as he patiently answered the many questions she fired at him. She showed him her new purse and shared her stash of gum.

"Do you have a cigarette in there, by any chance?" he asked. The look on Ruthie's face answered that silly question.

"Time to go," the stout old nun ordered.

Dad gave her one more hug, and then pulled something out of his pocket. "This is for your new purse. I only had a dollar to put in it, though." The beaded wallet Ruthie had admired in the gift shop window while Mom was signing the visitor's log was now hers.

Dad got back on the stretcher. The Sister covered him up, head to toe (leaving the toe tag hanging out) and turned the cart toward the elevator. Ruthie was relieved the nun was not going to the morgue with this patient.

As Ruthie waited for her mother to return, she thought about what had just occurred. Never in her strictly Protestant upbringing had she imagined that Catholic nuns could stray so far from the mental picture she had created of them in her mind—strict, mean, unbending, sinning only by accident, she was sure. Yet, this little nun had obviously broken many rules to make her birthday wish come true. Ruthie worried what the nun would say when she went to confession, which was something her friends apparently dreaded. She wondered if the priest would make her do penance. Ruthie wasn't sure what that was, but she had heard of it and was pretty sure it was not something good.

Ruthie remembered a lesson she had learned in Sunday school: Jesus said the greatest commandment was love. She recognized the intimidating nun may have broken the hospital rules, but she had certainly obeyed the highest rule of all in this circumstance.

Ruthie's golden eighth birthday did indeed shine. The gum disappeared first, the purse not long after. Her Dad recovered, and somehow her mother got them through that difficult winter. However, from that day forward, Ruthie kept an open mind, always remembering a birthday gift from a kindly nun.

*

Janice also had birthdays on her mind as she got ready for bed. She was grateful for each one she was privileged to celebrate and a relatively recent experience had left her with an appreciation for each day in between birthday celebrations, too.

Laura, Not Laurie

aura. Not Laurie. Her daughter was firm about that; only her brother or a stranger dared call her Laurie. It suited her, Janice thought, as she placed the photo on her scrapbook page. She looked so elegant in her prom dress, her figure slim and straight, every curl carefully coiffed, a touch of glitter across her shoulders. Even her nail polish perfectly complemented her dress and makeup. In Laura's mind, and her boyfriend's, the effect was no doubt worth the numerous shopping trips to the mall.

"Where is Polly?" asked Laura. "My friends are coming over."

She's too concerned about appearances, Janice thought, as she put the deckle scissors on the pile of scraps and sat back. 'Polly' was the wig she wore when out in public. The polyester disguise at least kept her head warm.

"My hair is growing back. Do I really need Polly?" her mother inquired.

"But, Mother, your hair is so curly and tight it looks like a scouring pad!" Laura exclaimed. "The wig is much more normal looking."

Normal. That was the key to life, she thought, as she tucked her bunny-slippered feet under the chair. They probably would have passed inspection but one ear had been chewed off by the dog and the left one wore a spot of fresh egg yolk.

"Are they coming to crop or just picking you up?"

"Oh, they're bringing their pictures. You have the coolest collection of scrapbook tools of anyone we know."

The Saturday morning sun spilled over the breakfast counter. Laura curled her slender fingers around the mug of hot chocolate with its lone marshmallow basking in steam. No clutter in Laura's world, not even in her cup. She would approach her scrapbook craft with discipline: a small bag taped to the table for her scraps, her various scissors and glues all neatly organized in a tool box.

Janice looked again at the photo of her daughter and her boyfriend standing before the backdrop of a beautiful scene complete with a miniature working water wheel slowly spilling water from bucket to bucket. She had been Laura's age when her mother had died from breast cancer. Yet, like the water steadily moving through the water wheel, life had gone on for her and her father. She knew that it would continue for Laura, too, if the cancer returned, and Laura would be left someday to scrapbook her wedding pictures without her mother.

What must I teach her today, she wondered? How do I balance the ordinary with the need to identify and recognize the extraordinary?

Laura opened her scrapbook and glanced at the layout she had sketched. She let her long auburn hair fall curtain-like in front of her face and studied her mother's work unobtrusively.

What can I learn from her today, she wondered? How do I balance my need to figure out things for myself yet take advantage of what she can teach me now?

They worked in silence, each crafting their relationship as carefully as the pages they worked to preserve as keepsakes.

Janice folded the memory away as she turned the bed covers back. Yes, she was grateful for every day with which she was graced.

Please Wait Here...

"I didn't realize tropical birds could be sighted this far north," Sam commented as he pulled his driver's cap a little lower over his twinkling brown eyes and leaned against the bus.

"Sam!" Emily exclaimed as she thrust her head out of the bus door to see what had prompted his remark.

Merry Terry slammed the motel room door and hurried toward the bus. Then she circled back to pick up the straw sandal she had stepped out of in her rush. Her apple green pants splashed randomly throughout with orange poppies were topped by a loose-fitting matching blouse. The straw hat did little to dim the sparse magenta hair trailing from its rim. A large tote hanging on one arm was offset by the large macramé purse hanging from her opposite shoulder. A wobbly wheel on her suitcase caused a serious list, which she attempted to correct by giving it a kick every other step.

"Well, at least she's not late this morning. I warned her that her travel companions were growing weary of that routine," Emily said.

"I'm growing weary of finding space in cargo for the things that seem to follow her after every stop we make."

"Sam, you have to admit it's nice to have a traveler who is perpetually cheerful instead of whining all the time. We've both experienced that a time or two."

"True, true. And I do have my sunglasses handy for when she gets too close."

"Good morning!" Terry sang out as she squeezed past Emily and looked for an empty seat. Terry was traveling as a single on this tour, which no doubt contributed to her tardiness. But she had no problem finding a seat partner—her sunny disposition was generally welcomed and she was quick to spot and avoid the non-morning people. They did, however, insist that she never again hum "The Wheels on the Bus Go Round and Round." No one wanted that tune traveling with them all day. Settling into an aisle seat, she opened her tote and reached for glasses.

"Wait! I can't find my glasses!" Terry called out to the bus driver.

Sam was expecting it. "Check your pockets, Terry."

"Oh, thanks, they're right here."

Sam pulled the bus onto the highway. Another day was underway.

Just outside of town they came to a sudden, unexpected stop.

"What was that?" Emily asked, leaning forward so her voice could be heard over the excited murmurs behind her.

"A flat tire," he replied. Pulling into a curved gravel driveway that framed a huge yard filled with lawn and garden ornaments and statuary for sale, he turned off the engine and set the parking brake.

"Everyone off, please," he directed, while releasing the right front of the bus to its kneeling position. The older ladies in particular appreciated this feature of the bus, as it narrowed considerably the distance from the bottom step to the ground.

When they had gathered outside in an excited huddle Emily addressed them. "Ladies, your attention, please." She waited for the chatter to quiet and continued. "We expect the repair to take about an hour. The sun is warming quickly so you may want to get your water bottles and whatever else you want from the bus now. Once the road crew arrives we will not be able to re-board the bus until the tire is changed. Feel free to wander the nearby area but stay within calling distance, please."

The women dispersed among the bird baths and garden bells and gazing globes to make good use of the opportunity this distraction provided.

"Look at these stepping stones," Ruth said as she kneeled to inspect them more closely. "This darling bunny is a key safe. My grandchildren would love this."

"Yeah, but it wouldn't fool a thief," Betty replied. "They'll spot that in a minute."

"I could put one of those old-fashioned antique keys in it and the kids could pretend it opens the shed. They are young enough to believe the key really is unlocking that old door."

Betty chuckled. "Why not have your husband put a false bottom in your bird feeder, too? Then you could leave a secret message for them to find or maybe plant a clue to find treasure buried in the garden."

"Oh, they would absolutely love that. Maybe I'll plan something like that for Halloween, since the schools these days aren't allowed to provide the kind of fun we used to have on holidays."

Betty raised her eyebrows at that information. "Why ever not?" she asked. Her only contact with elementary schools in recent times was to go there to vote.

"Political correctness, I guess. The only way to make sure they include everyone and offend no one is to do nothing."

Lois had been enjoying their conversation as she examined the gaudy dancing Dutch kid statues nearby. Wandering away from Betty and Ruth, she strolled further down the path until she was stopped by a low, paint-peeled wooden fence that carved a thin line between the commercial property and a cemetery on the other side. Spotting a gate a few feet away, Lois nudged it open and stepped inside. She tied her sweater around her slim waist and gazed at the peaceful scene before her.

A slight breeze whispered through the pines overhead as if to remind her that this was a place of solitude. Wiping the warmth from her forehead, she folded her tall frame down on a bench set in a plot reserved for military burials. Red and white silk carnations stood guard in bronze vases at each grave and small flags marked the headstones. Staring at the date of death on the stone near her feet, in the hard granite reflection her mind began to see a memory from long ago. Resting her head in her hands, she took time to relive that hour out of respect for those at her feet today.

What Did You Learn in School Today?

Thirty-two pairs of eyes stared out the window and one pair stared straight ahead, four inches to the left of the clock on the back wall of the classroom. Momentarily Mr. Thompson took his eyes off the spot on the back wall to pull down the map of Greece.

She watched as the doors opened on the hearse across the parking lot next to the church. The shared lot that was normally filled with student junker cars now held much nicer cars with small purple flags flying somberly from their hoods. Six young men surrounded the flag-draped casket and prepared to carry it into the church.

They should have been thinking about how the coastal configuration of Greece shaped its economy. Instead, they were thinking how cruel it was for the September sun to shine so brilliantly on such a dark day. Stained glass was scattered sparsely throughout the array of windows on the church. The clear glass gave an un-shadowed view of the solemn procession to the altar.

She saw a flash of red in the reflection of the hearse. It reminded her of the last time she saw James A. Johannssen, now deceased. It was just last spring, right before his graduation from the very school where she now sat, very much alive. He was in her father's sport shop and she was selling him his graduation present: a 50 cc Harley-Davidson motorcycle, in bright shiny Christmas red.

"I won't be 18 until next week so I will have to bring my Dad back with me to sign the papers," he said, leaning his long frame against the counter.

"That's okay. I'm not old enough to officially sell it to you, anyway, but my Dad will be here when you return." She concentrated on being very business-like and professional about this big sale and suppressed any indication of her secret crush on this football hero. "You'll really enjoy your new bike this summer." She briefly pictured herself hanging on tightly to his waist, black ponytail flying in the wind as the motorcycle spun down a curvy country road.

"It will be a short one, but sweet," he replied.

The warm, sweet fragrance of chocolate filled the air. They were baking brownies in Home Economics class across the hall. The normally comforting smell was numbing now. It simply underscored the briefness of pleasant things, such as life and innocence and childhood.

The classroom seemed unnaturally still. Mr. Thompson apparently couldn't think of a single question to ask them today. To the back wall, four inches to the left of the clock, he gave an earnest lecture on some Greek battle. The students gave inward attention to the war in Vietnam.

The toll of the church bell chimed along with the buzzer that ended this awful hour. They gathered their books and filed silently out the door. Today they learned that they were mortal.

Brushing the dust from her long flowered skirt, Lois rose from the cool bench and glanced back at the group. The women were beginning to find their way back to the bus. They must be ready to roll, she thought, as she closed the gate behind her and picked her way back through the bird baths and sundials.

"Madam, you simply cannot take the gargoyle on the bus." Sam was adamant. "Aside from being totally hideous, it is simply too big. It will get damaged in the cargo hold and it's downright dangerous to anyone else on the bus." Sam eyed the pointed teeth and evil grin of the statue's curled lips.

"It is not hideous. This is art, for goodness' sake." Karen was equally adamant as she hugged the tall, ungainly creature tightly to her chest.

"She'll never find anything like it again," Amy added.

"Well, that's a good thing, I think," replied Sam.

Emily stepped in. "We all know beauty is in the eye of the beholder," she said, giving Sam a sharp look. Arguing with the tour guests was seldom productive.

"I know how to solve this," Terry chimed in. "Have the owners ship it home for you. They will pack it right and tight for you, I'm sure of it." Terry stepped back while subtly pushing her tote behind her broad back. No need to draw attention to the homey, hand-painted 'The Ducks Stop Here' sign peeking from its top.

"I suppose that is the best answer," Karen reluctantly agreed. "I really do have the perfect spot for this in my landscape."

Sam climbed into the driver's seat. He could just imagine the perfect spot: the garbage curb.

Tea on the Veranda

arianne rocked gently in the big white rocker on the veranda of the Grand Hotel on Mackinac Island. Stirring sugar into her tall glass of iced tea, she looked discreetly around her to see what the other tea guests were wearing. Glancing down at her deep blue sweater, carefully buttoned all the way to the top, she adjusted the collar of the crisp white blouse and straightened the pearl necklace around her throat. Matching blue cropped pants with embroidered flowers around the wide hem stopped just above her sensible walking shoes. Satisfied that her attire blended in with the vacation clothes she observed on those around her, she released the reigns on her nervousness and began to relax. Marianne never wanted to stand out or draw attention.

Normally, her frugal nature and lifelong practice of penny-pinching would have overruled her desire to sit on a rocking chair on the grand porch of a graceful old hotel. The ten-dollar cost seemed quite extravagant to her and she didn't know how she would explain to her husband that she was spending money so foolishly, if she even told him.

The server placed a freshly prepared tray of treats on the wicker table between the rockers. Reaching for a cranberry scone, Marianne let the sweet fragrance take her back to her own kitchen for a moment. She loved to bake. Cookies, cakes, bars, pies—anything requiring time in the oven provided her with a respite from the daily chores necessary to keeping a house clean and orderly and her family fed and content. Kneading dough and patiently waiting for it to rise seemed to help her let go of the little frustrations and disappointments that collected like dust on a knick knack if not attended to regularly.

She thought about the hidden Marianne this trip seemed to be bringing out. Perhaps it was the sense of safety and security she got from being with other women and seeing the freedom they felt in trying new things. Or maybe habitually subjugating her own choices for those of her family over the years had brought her to a stopping point. She hoped that whatever key unlocked her self-discipline, it would stay lost until this trip was over. She knew that once she returned to her normal environment, the Marianne she was used to would slip back into the role that shaped her life.

Marianne was certain that the source of funding for today's pleasure would remain untold to her family and friends. That night at the casino in Manistique she had intended only to watch the others, knowing she'd never be in a casino again in her life. Everything in her upbringing railed against such activity. Everything in her family and friendships precluded behavior that was risky or questionable. Everything in her own moral code ensured that her feet would follow the straight and narrow path they had always walked.

So what had possessed her for one hour that night to put all the spare change in her purse into slot machines? She thought it was born more of curiosity than rebellion,

although she readily confessed to not really thinking it
through at all. Never one to be impulsive, something had
allowed her fingers to snap open that clasp and fish for
coins. Something had quieted her ever-alert conscience for
a moment while she slipped into an open chair before a
brightly colored machine. Something about the sound of
money gushing into the slot when the three cherries lined
up across the pay line kept her there to pull the handle
again.

Her wild abandon that hour netted her $200. A little pin
money, her grandmother would have called it. Maybe that's
where she got that tiny spark of courage to act outside of
herself. In any case, it was money that her husband hadn't
known about before this trip and wouldn't know about
after. He would never again let her go anywhere by herself
if he thought she couldn't be trusted to act responsibly. But
she might tell him about the breeze blowing through her
short, white hair as she rocked on the porch of the beautiful
Grand Hotel. He just didn't need to know that the relaxing
treat wasn't free. After all, she hadn't endured over forty
years of marriage without developing the art of skillful
explanation.

"Care for company?" Emily asked as she dropped into a
rocker next to Marianne.

"Sure, Emily—what good is tea without conversation?"
Marianne picked up the plate of sweets and offered it to
Emily. She restrained herself from popping up to search for
a server. "I'm sure someone will stop by soon to get you a
beverage."

Marianne, eager to guide the conversation lest her most
recent thoughts suddenly find expression, nodded toward
the Mackinac Bridge shimmering in the distance.
"Mackinac makes me think of the musical Brigadoon—it is
simply enchanting," she commented.

"Fortunately, it won't disappear when we leave," Emily laughed. "I have been here when the fog enshrouds everything and sometimes you'll just see the peaks of the bridge arching above the clouds. That gives it a much more sinister fascination, I think." Emily slipped off her sandals and tucked her feet under her legs on the spacious rocker.

"Have you traveled a lot of places, then?" Marianne questioned.

"I have and I haven't. I'd been to many places on work-related assignments before I became a tour director but I didn't see those places from a tourist's point of view. I was so caught up in the work that I barely noticed my surroundings, other than figuring out how to get places on time."

"Why would you become a tour director? It seems like you're always on the job now, too."

Emily thought about that before replying. "It's different. In this job, travel is the assignment, so I am focused on my surroundings and the people I'm with during the tour. This travel is about the people, not about giving a high-pressure presentation or gathering information to analyze when you get back home. Northern Experience Tours offers different tours such as this one, the Dream Catcher Tour, that keep it interesting for me. Have you traveled a lot, Marianne?"

"Goodness, no—I almost never leave my home territory. My family insisted I sign up for this tour just to get me out of Cedarburg for once."

Emily carefully lifted the bone china teacup to her lips. The Victorian Earl Grey tea was still steaming. "Cedarburg?"

"Wisconsin," Marianne smiled.

"Tell me what it is like to be so home-centered. Did you ever have a job besides home-making?" Emily had been an army brat and frequent moves throughout her dad's career meant there was nowhere that she really considered home. It was more of a concept to her than a geographic location.

Marianne laid her precisely folded napkin back on the tray and lifted her soft blue eyes to meet Emily's. "I love keeping my home up to the old German standards I was raised with, but every now and then I want to have a little extra money to help out with the family budget. I have a neighbor who has a little beauty salon in her basement and during her busy times, like holidays and the prom and wedding seasons, I wash hair for her."

Turning the conversation back to Emily, she asked, "Why do you choose to guide tours to the Upper Peninsula? I would think someone as sophisticated as you would choose a foreign country or at least a state far away from the Midwest."

Oh, if only she knew how unsophisticated I really am, thought Emily. But she suppressed her brief insecurity and responded.

"I love the people and the beauty of this place. My grandparents lived in Escanaba and I spent many happy vacations exploring the towns up here with them. My grandfather was a history teacher and I was his favorite student on those trips. I really enjoy sharing my knowledge and love of this peninsula with people who have never been here before, or maybe haven't been here for many years. And I know that we will always be welcomed because friendliness runs as deep in these people as the roots of those trees into the earth."

"Have you ever been on the other side of that mighty bridge?" Marianne asked.

"Okay, here's a little secret—I had a friend I played with on my vacations up here who told me that people who lived below the bridge were trolls. I was fifteen before I crossed the Mackinac Bridge and I was greatly relieved to find that the people were every bit as friendly as the Yoopers."

"I suppose your friend told you to bait the trolls with fudge so they would like you?" Marianne joked.

"Hey, when did a little chocolate ever hurt?"

Emily uncurled her legs and eased her feet back into her sandals. "You are right, Marianne—I am always on the job and it's time to see what the quarreling sisters are up to now. I seem to have developed a mother's ear for sensing trouble among her own. Those definitely aren't wind chimes I hear farther down the veranda."

Marianne leaned back onto the brightly flowered cushion and closed her eyes, dozing off to a scene of little trolls sitting around her kitchen table charmingly begging for just one more double-fudge brownie.

Flutter-Bys

"*To make a wish come true, whisper it to a butterfly. Upon these wings it will be taken to Heaven and granted. For they are the messengers of the Great Spirit. —Native American Folklore*," Leslie read from the brochure in her hand. They were standing in the airlock entrance to the Butterfly House on Mackinac Island.

"Aunt Helen, when I was little I kept mixing up my words and I called them flutter-bys. I still think that's a better name for these lovely little creatures."

Aunt Helen simply nodded and stepped through the second door of the airlock, following the strains of classical music to the fairyland inside.

Emily turned to Leslie. "Oh, how enchanting!" she exclaimed.

Her senses were filled with the sights and sounds in the bubble surrounding her. Hundreds of butterflies flitted from flower to branch to ledge, accompanied by the sound of gentle waterfalls and soft orchestral strings flowing from hidden speakers. Even the children seemed to take their cue from the fragile insects and muted their chatter to their best interpretation of an indoor voice.

"Is this your first visit to a butterfly house, Emily?" Leslie asked. "Surely this isn't a new experience for you?"

"Actually, it is. There are always so many choices to make during the free time on a tour and somehow I've missed this option on my past trips."

"Aunt Helen adores animals of just about every kind, so we never miss a zoo or an exhibit or conservation park of any kind," Leslie laughed.

"Okay—you said 'almost' every kind. What's the exception?"

"Reptiles, of course. She understands their purpose in creation, but doesn't need to observe it personally."

Leslie looked around for her dear friend and spotted her kneeling over a low stone wall examining a feeder hanging from a low branch. A small child sat cross-legged beside her. Leslie knew they would soon be conspiring on how to get the big blue butterfly resting on the feeder to open its iridescent wings for them.

"Do you go on many trips with your aunt, Leslie?" Emily had noticed how comfortably they traveled together.

"Not as many as I did before I had a career. Now it's a little tougher to take time off for these trips. Business is a difficult and demanding master."

The butterfly world disappeared and was momentarily replaced in Emily's mind by a nest of cubicles with ringing phones and clattering keyboards. Perhaps she had found a kindred spirit in Leslie. Dare she indulge in getting to know her better?

"Look!" Leslie exclaimed. "They are flying in formation."

Emily glanced at the butterflies crossing above her like geese flying south. "I'm sure that is a coincidence," she laughed. "I do know that butterflies don't live long enough to develop any collaboration skills."

"True, they do have a pretty short life span. I hope they make the most of it."

Ah, the burning question flared to life for Emily once again. If she had less than a year to live the rest of her life, how would she spend the time? Why was it so important to her to answer that question? Was this questioning yet another sign of ever-creeping age stealing her peace and casting shadows over her thoughts? She had thought only men went through a mid-life crisis.

"Leslie, I am getting to like your flutter-by word more and more. These insects remind me that life does seem to fly by in a flutter and if you close your eyes too long, you will miss it."

"Oh, I think that applies more to the good times. I've sat in meetings that seemed like they would consume many lifetimes of a butterfly and there was nothing pretty about them, either."

Emily chuckled. She again felt that sense of a kindred spirit. Leaning towards a monarch balanced on a wispy fern, she whispered her wish: I want to get to know Leslie a lot better.

That evening the sun slanted its rays across the dock. Emily stood at the entrance to the line of people waiting to board the ferry for St. Ignace, clipboard in hand. Terry calmly waited at her elbow, naming her tour buddies to Emily as she spotted them in the crowd. Emily clicked each one on the counter she kept on a brightly braided lanyard around her neck. It was an invaluable aid to her in keeping track of her forty-seven women.

"Only four more to arrive and I'm not one of them," Terry smiled up at Emily.

"No, you've been very prompt today. We are still missing the Fearsome 4Sum. They walked up to the Wawashkamo Golf Club and I think it was further than they expected."

"They do love their golf, don't they?" Terry commented.

Sun-kissed day trippers continued to board the ferry. Guiding her aunt to a shaded bench on the lower deck, Leslie fished a windbreaker out of her backpack and handed it to her. Slicing through the waves in the high-speed catamaran would quickly cool their bare arms.

Joining Emily on the upper deck, Leslie leaned on the railing and watched the island slowly diminish in the distance. "I'm a little concerned about Aunt Helen," she began. "She just doesn't seem herself."

"What makes you think that?" Emily inquired. "I don't know her as well as you do, of course. Don't you think she's enjoying herself?" Emily took Leslie's remark seriously since it was her primary job responsibility to ensure that all of the guests of Northern Experience Tours got the most out of their trip experience.

"She seems to be more tired than I've seen her. It's just not like her to be sitting on a bench with her eyes closed instead of hovering over the captain's shoulder peppering him with questions."

"Well, all that fresh air and gorgeous sunshine we took advantage of today does tend to tire a body," Emily replied, "to say nothing of the generous fudge samples we were compelled to try."

"I suppose. You're right—I am reading too much into it."

Terry rushed by twirling a Detroit Tiger's baseball cap in her stubby fingers.

"Obviously the sun and fresh air didn't put a dent in *her* energy," Leslie smiled.

No, Emily thought as she wove her way among the passengers, Merry Terry had energy for them all. The last four women on her passenger list were now on board. She found a seat and rested her arms against the bench back to enjoy the short ride to the peninsula.

Sam tugged the bus door closed and pulled the bus out of the ferry parking lot. Drawing the microphone down, he announced in his deep voice, "One hour to Sault Ste Marie, ladies. We will be staying at a very comfortable hotel tonight."

The women tucked their bags into the overhead bins and settled into their seats, glad to be off their feet for a while. This would be a quiet ride, Emily thought, as she put her clipboard in her messenger bag and reclined her seat. And there would be some evening left to enjoy in Sault Ste. Marie.

Fore

Emily paid for her drink at the Open Season bar and walked over to the curved corner table where the Fearsome 4Sum were seated.

"Room for another one?" she asked.

"Of course, Emily," replied Madeline as she slid over to make room on the bench. "Need a little nightcap, too?"

"Yes, I guess so," she laughed. "It has been a long day. But I'm just not quite ready to let it end."

She looked around at the rough planked walls of the rustic bar. Antlers were screwed to nearly every available space. Sports pictures occupied occasional spaces in between the antlers and all sports were amply represented. Hockey of course dominated, but that was to be expected in The Soo, and a picture of a beautiful golf hole hung just above Maggie's head.

"So, tell me how you four came to be known as the Fearsome 4Sum."

After the laughter quieted down, Maggie answered. "Three of us are teachers in the same school district back home and Lynn is a Gray Lady Volunteer in my school. Madeline teaches Social Studies, Amy is a Language Arts teacher, and I teach Math. We all love to play golf and decided to join a ladies' league at our local Rolling Ridge Country Club. We still hadn't decided on a name for our group the first night of league play and we had to come up with something by the end of the round.

The fairway on the first hole is divided by a water hazard and the geese love to hang out along that area. They are used to the golfers so they don't generally move out of the way. Well, my tee shot didn't quite get enough height on it and the ball hit a goose. There was a grounds keeper waiting for us to get out of the way so he could move the sprinkler. When he saw the goose react to being hit, he made a remark about staying out of the way of the 'fearsome foursome.' Maddie quickly converted 'foursome' to '4Sum' and that's what we entered in the league ledger."

Emily laughed. "Very clever, girls, although I would expect teachers to come up with something creative like that. I have to ask, though—are you really fearsome on the golf course?"

Amy coughed as laughter bubbled up while she was trying to swallow her beer. Lynn patted her on the back and Maggie grabbed a napkin to catch the beer that splashed out of Amy's mug when she slapped it on the table. It was now inching towards the edge of the table to create a beer hazard in someone's lap.

Madeline calmly answered. "Of course we are fearsome, but more for the weird things that seem to occur while we are on the course than for our golfing ability."

Emily took the bait. "What weird things?"

The Fearsome 4Sum looked at each other. "Where do we begin?" Lynn questioned over the blare of the country western song playing from the jukebox.

"Well, there was the time that Maddie hit her ball into the rough and decided it was playable. When she took her backswing, her club hit a bee's nest in the tree branch above her head and woke up a bunch of angry insects," Maggie responded.

"And the tournament two summers ago, when each hole had a different challenge and we had to hit our drives blindfolded. Amy, even though she's as tall as she is, seemed to think it would take a lot more speed to hit a ball blindfolded—she swung so hard she fell right over. Plus, she missed the ball," Lynn contributed.

"Another round, ladies?" the young man serving their table asked.

Emily looked at the Pink Squirrel in front of her. "I'm fine, thanks." One ice cream drink was plenty for her.

"You can bring us one more pitcher," Amy announced for the group. "We have more stories than beer at this point."

"Hand me that antler on the ledge," Madeline ordered. "I need a talking stick. We can't forget the round when Lynn drove the cart into the creek."

Emily turned to stare at Lynn. "How on earth could you do that?"

Lynn stared morosely into her beer. "I was afraid."

Madeline tossed her head back and laughed. "Lynn, you are the most intimidating-looking person I know when you want to be, and you can handle any situation. I still find it hard to believe that a little green grass snake can have that kind of power over you."

"I'll take ten lunchroom bullies on in a minute over a snake. And it wasn't little and it wasn't green. Besides, it's hard to drive when you have your feet up on the steering wheel and you're screaming. I only have so much coordination, you know."

Emily stood up. "I think I'm ready to pack it in now. Thanks for the entertainment, girls. I hope you enjoy many more happy rounds of golf together."

"And then there was the time we were caught in that thunderstorm…" Lynn continued reminiscing as Emily picked her way through the crowded tables to the entrance. She paused when she spotted Terry sitting alone, deeply engrossed in the baseball game playing on the wide screen mounted above the bar.

"Drinking alone?" she asked.

Terry twisted back and spotted Emily in the crowd behind her. "Nope—not drinking and not alone," she stated as she opened her arms to indicate the people around her. "It's just a soft drink. I love to watch the games on big screens so I thought I'd catch the ending here."

"Since you are smiling, I will assume your team is winning," Emily commented.

"I watch them, winning or not. Ya gotta stick by your team."

Emily let that thought accompany her back to the hotel. She could feel the team camaraderie developing among the women on this tour and enjoyed being a part of it.

*

The next morning dawned overcast and cool. Mary glanced at the rain-laden clouds and decided that exploring the shops along the main street would be a suitably dry activity. She had passed up the freighter tour since boats of any size were of no interest to her. Shopping, however, could hold her attention for many hours, especially shopping in curiosity and gift shops.

A Christmas tree painted on a shop sign swinging gently above a store caught her eye. That will be my first stop, she thought as she waited for the walk signal to light up. Mary had a passion for all things Christmas.

"May I help you?" inquired the sales assistant.

"Just looking, thank you," Mary replied as she took in the store layout. Christmas trees crowded the wall to her left, all lit and decorated in various themes. Directly in front of her were tables filled with ornaments of all kinds. On her right were garlands and a wide assortment of yard decorations. Strolling past the tables to the shelves filled with knick knacks, Mary brushed a rack of ponchos and scarves. She paused as a memory suddenly surfaced. Family and friends were the primary reason she loved the Christmas season and the scarves reminded her of a very special friend from her childhood.

She headed to the snack bar at the back of the store. "One hot caramel apple cider coffee," she ordered. A hot drink would hit the spot on this unseasonably chilly day. Settling onto a stool, she let her mind drift back to a Christmas many years past.

Christmas Swans

They shared something with each other before they even met. Mary was a new student in the fourth grade that November and there were no places left to hang her coat. She was told to hang it in Grace's locker. Grace was in the hospital with pneumonia and Mary remembered making a get well card for her as part of a class assignment that day. She worried that she didn't know how to spell 'anxious', among other things.

Grace was nice enough to share her locker space with Mary for the rest of that year. Now it was November again and they were in the ninth grade, still sharing a locker—this time out of choice rather than necessity.

"This snow sure launches the Christmas season!" Grace said as she shook the snow out of her hat.

"Yes, now that Thanksgiving is over, it's time to start planning," Mary agreed.

"And earning!" Grace replied.

That set Mary thinking. Now that she was in high school, babysitting opportunities were more plentiful and she was beginning to get regular customers. Grace was the eldest of seven children and all her babysitting was done at home for free. In the summer, Grace collected lost golf balls on the course near her home and sold them—but what would she do in winter?

By the time school was out the snow had turned to slush and Mary's Christmas spirit was sagging. Nevertheless, Grace was enthusiastically waving a list about.

"I did it during Algebra. I wrote down all the names and ideas of what to get them. I've budgeted a dollar per person. I'm going to make some of the gifts," Grace confided. With that, she ran out to catch her bus while Mary headed to the band room to pick up her French horn. She wasn't really planning to practice it, but if she brought it home it was an excuse for her Dad to give her a ride to school in the morning. She didn't mind the walk in the afternoon, though, and as she headed for home she began making a mental list of the people on her Christmas list.

The next morning Grace had her book bag, clarinet and another bag too big to be her lunch.

"Are you staying in town tonight?" Mary asked.

"Yes, at Grandma's," replied Grace. "Do you want to go shopping after school?"

"Sure," she answered hurriedly. The first bell was about to ring and homeroom was a long way away. "See you in band," she said.

"We are going to begin a unit on the short story. There are several authors famous for their short stories and the one we shall study is O. Henry," Mr. Carlson said as he lounged against the edge of his desk. I liked Mr. Carlson.

"We are going to read several of his stories to get the idea of the pattern of the short story. Your assignment is to read one story by O. Henry. And yes, that means library work," he continued. Mr. Carlson expected research.

Mary had her books packed and ready to go by the time the bell rang so she could beat the crowd to the library. She dashed in, picked up the first book she could find by O. Henry, and headed for her locker. Grace was waiting.

"I hope you have your homework done," she said as Mary approached.

"All except English," Mary replied.

They quickly stuffed books into the locker and started for downtown. The gray skies now offered, instead of gloom, a quiet contrast to the growing Christmas excitement within them.

"What are you going to get everybody?" Mary asked Grace as they waited for a break in traffic to cross the street.

"I'm going to make rag dolls for my sisters and drum sets for my brothers. For my Mom I'll make some jewelry and maybe a tie for my Dad. I don't know yet about my grandparents," Grace replied.

"How are you going to pay for the supplies?"

"Last night I searched in the woods for some pieces of log. I'm going to buy some candles and get some pine boughs and make centerpieces decorated with ribbon. Then I'm going to sell them to my neighbors."

"That's a great idea," Mary enthused. "I'll buy one from you—that would take care of one person on my list."

They threaded their way through the aisles of Christmas things—tree trimmings, toys, perfumes and scarves—to the food counter. There were no stools left so they leaned against the magazine rack and checked their financial resources. They each had enough for one soft drink, but Mary knew Grace wanted to save money for her Christmas shopping so she offered to share hers. Christmas carols filled the air and they could see the Salvation Army woman standing on the corner just outside the store ringing her bell earnestly in spite of the cold. The Christmas feeling of giving expanded.

The next day Mary settled down to discover what O. Henry had to offer. Mr. Carlson handed out a copy of a story and began reading. 'The Gift of the Magi' was about a young couple that dearly loved one another but was very poor and had no money to buy Christmas gifts. In order to get extra money, the girl sacrificed her beautiful hair and sold it. She bought her husband a fine chain for his beloved watch. The husband, meanwhile, pawned his watch to buy a lovely set of combs for his wife's beautiful hair.

The class discussion was very interesting. Some thought it was sad that each had given up treasured possessions and some, naturally, thought the story was stupid. Mary thought it was wonderful that these two people had put their feelings for each other above their feelings for their favorite possessions.

The thought of sacrificing so that you had something to give put a new perspective on her idea of giving. She guessed she'd always thought you gave of what you had and if you didn't have anything extra, you didn't give anything. Perhaps she had some more to learn about giving.

Another question bothered Mary. Mr. Carlson said the two people in the story were 'Magi' because they were wise givers. Are there any wise givers today, he wondered?

These thoughts, however, were quickly pushed aside as she entered the choir room. Today they got their choir robes. The holiday concert was coming soon and they had a lot of practicing yet to do.

The picture of the little man in the corner of the daily newspaper announced only five more shopping days until Christmas. Only three more school days! The rush of Christmas activities meant that interest in schoolwork was low and excitement in everything else was high.

On the last afternoon of school before vacation, they met in the auditorium for the annual Christmas assembly.

The choir sang, the band played, and various faculty members entertained. Mary thoroughly enjoyed the program. When it was over, she and Grace threaded their way through the crowded hallways to their locker. She was suddenly touched with sadness that the season she had so eagerly anticipated was already reaching its peak and soon would be but a memory. Grace was busy packing her things into their locker—her bus driver didn't wait for anyone! Before she hurried down the hallway, she turned and handed Mary a package, saying softly, "Merry Christmas!" She was gone before Mary could even thank her.

When she recovered from her surprise, she put down her books and opened the package. It was a beautiful white scarf decorated with graceful blue swans dancing along each end. She had admired it many times while window shopping, but only mentioned it once that first day she and Grace had shopped together.

"I've budgeted a dollar per person," echoed through her mind. She realized that allowing a dollar for a gift for her meant Grace considered her to be equal to a member of her own family. Mary was overwhelmed.

"Are there any wise givers today?" Mr. Carlson had asked. The halls were empty now, but right after vacation, Mary would be sure to tell him that she knew of one.

*

The chime of the cuckoo clock on the wall startled Mary back to the present. Pulling her purse over her shoulder, she slid off the stool and walked to the rack displaying the colorful scarves. No—no dancing blue swans among the snowmen and elves.

Smiling to herself, Mary selected a souvenir ornament for her Christmas tree and took it to the sales counter. She turned to the door at the sound of the unique door chime. It played a short drum roll each time someone walked through the door between the two life-size nutcrackers that guarded the entrance.

"Sandy?" she asked. "Enjoying your shopping?"

"Oh, yes, there are some delightful gift shops in this town," replied Sandy. "I'm sure the tour of the Soo Locks would have been interesting, too, but somehow it's easier to forget it's raining on one of your vacation days when you're shopping."

"That's true, although I love to shop no matter what the weather."

Sandy waited for Mary to pay for her souvenir. "Would you like to find a place to have lunch?" she asked as they left the checkout counter.

"But you just got here—don't you want to look around first?" Mary inquired. "We have plenty of time."

"I was really looking for someone to have lunch with," Sandy said. "I spotted you through that winter wonderland window and thought it would be nice to enjoy lunch with you. So I guess I did find what I was looking for," she smiled.

The drum rolled as they walked out the door together. Pausing under the awning, Mary looked up and down the street. "I think we'll come to the Freighter View restaurant if we head down this street. I've heard it's a very good place to eat."

"Plus, there are a couple more stores that look appealing along the way," Sandy said as she pulled up the hood on her rain jacket.

*

Sam pulled past the Porta Potties on the pickup truck ahead of him into the passing lane. He suspected they were a sign of the afternoon ahead of them. Finally, he thought, as he peered through the driving rain and located the edge line of the lane in the spray of mist. He caught Emily's nod and pressed the start button. Emily had chosen 'Calendar Girls' for the movie today. It seemed perfect for the rainy afternoon ride to Munising. She hoped the weather would clear for their stop at Tahquamenon Falls.

This movie was always a popular choice and one that Emily didn't mind seeing again. Mentally tuning out the sound, she opened her tour guide notebook and recorded the receipts she had collected over the past couple of days. There was a fair amount of administrative work associated with guiding tours and the discipline she had taken from her previous career served her well now.

Turning to the journal section of her notebook, Emily paused to think about what to write. She used this section as a place to note the lessons she had learned from her group so that she could incorporate them into future tours. This was the first time she had escorted a women-only group, so she had a lot of new observations. Usually at least two or three men tagged along.

She thought of Leslie. She knew that it was her responsibility as tour director to ensure that all participants enjoyed their experience, so she was careful to rotate throughout the group and spend time with each person. In fact, that was one of the most enjoyable aspects of her job. Her conversation with Leslie at the butterfly house yesterday, however, had sparked her interest, and instinct told her the seeds of a friendship had taken root.

Emily quickly flipped back to her time chart and studied it carefully. With forty-seven women on board, the only fair way to make sure she didn't overlook anyone was to track her time spent with each one—another habit from her previous career that helped in her current role. The chart was a simple affair; noting the number of dots next to each name, she realized she had actually spent very little time with Leslie and her Aunt Helen.

Emily returned her notebook to the black canvas bag and sat back to enjoy the rest of the movie. As she let herself be drawn into the lives of the characters, she watched for ways in which these women approached their individual aging issues. As usual, she was on alert for new perspectives.

Barb gazed out at the steady rain as the images from the movie faded from her mind. She thought about the two years she had spent in England with her husband when he had been on the international rung of the corporate ladder. Two bitter years, she recalled...

Mind the Gap

"**M**ind the gap," the automated voice warned.

"Mind the gap between your ears," Roger said to his wife as the underground train doors snapped shut behind them.

"You'd best mind the gap in your face—we are not through with this discussion," Barbara replied.

"I don't know how many times we have to review this decision. He's going to St. Paul's Academy and that is the end of it."

"He's not going to be influenced by a bunch of aristocrats-in-the-making. He's an American and we are only here for another year before your foreign assignment is done."

"We are in England. I want him to learn every aspect of the culture and get the best education possible. He will never get an opportunity like this again."

"It is not fair to him to get him started in a fancy public school only to pull him out in another year."

"That makes no sense. We'll have to pull him out of any school we start him in after a year, unless you plan to leave him here until he graduates."

"That is unthinkable!" she replied, before murmuring, "Lower your voice, people are staring."

"They aren't staring at us," he said, nodding towards the couple behind them. "They're trying to figure out which sex is which in that embrace."

The train jerked to a stop and people shuffled to the doors.

"Mind the gap," the automated voice warned as the doors slid open.

"The gap in cultures is just too great for Robbie to manage in a blue-blood school," she continued. "He'll spend more time adjusting socially than learning anything in his classes. You may think you come from an uppity family, but even the highest born in America are given little respect here—you see that regularly in your job. No matter what you think, you are from the working class."

"No matter what *you* think, I am proud of my career and I want our son to have every advantage possible. Think of the prestige this education will bring to his future resume. He's going to St. Paul's."

"King's Cross," the automated attendant announced. People pushed between them toward the doors and the gap between the couple grew.

Barbara grabbed the strap overhead and squeezed into the corner. "Robbie's only thirteen years old. That's just too young for boarding school. His happiness is more important than a line on his resume. Who will care ten years from now?"

"Robin needs the discipline of a prep school far more than you need to keep him your little boy. He has to grow up sometime and there's no better place than a prep school," Roger stated. "He's already got the experience of living in a different culture. I simply want to enhance that experience."

"Oxford Circus. Mind the gap." The doors clicked open.

"Roger, look at us. We ride the Tube to our jobs every day. There is no way our son will adjust to an elite school atmosphere. You are handing him a challenge beyond his capacity."

"He will manage, and it will be the best thing for him. We've done well for ourselves but I want a better life for him. That means sacrificing some of our time with him now."

They departed the train and rode the escalator to the street. Roger turned left and flowed into the foot traffic while Barbara turned right, her thoughts blurring with the sights and sounds of the work day stretching before her.

*

Barb turned from the rain-streaked bus window, surprised that the old argument still bit so sharply into her memory. Gently pulling at the tape on the package in her lap, she folded back the tissue paper and lifted out the wall hanging. It was made of black wrought iron, a chickadee perched on a slender branch with three vivid red berries clinging like tear drops to a twig. She had found it at the Gift Haus at their last stop and was drawn to the fragile beauty set in a web of strength.

"Where shall I hang it?" she spoke softly to herself.

"Pardon me?" Linda asked from the seat next to her.

"Hmm? Oh, I'm sorry—I didn't realize I had spoken out loud."

"That's a beautiful wall hanging, Barb. Do you have a place in mind for it or was it just irresistible?"

Barb flashed a quiet smile. "I was just thinking about that. It was an impulsive purchase, and I don't regret that, but now I need to either find a place to hang it or think of someone to give it to."

Linda nodded, then opened her magazine and went back to work on the crossword puzzle.

Barb carefully tucked tissue paper around the chickadee and packed it back into its box. Perhaps Linda would find it a relatively simple matter to find a suitable place for a wall hanging, but for Barb it was a taste of freedom to be savored.

After thirty-two years as a faithful corporate warrior wife, she now found herself released from its rigid structure. She had signed up for the Dream Catcher Tour as a first tentative step into the world of self-determination and buying a wall hanging that tickled her fancy had been harder than she had anticipated.

Thinking about the other women on the bus, she observed that none of her traveling companions were young, twenty-something, shiny female trophies to be captured by wayward men who loved their careers more than anything or anyone else.

"I need to dispel these gloomy thoughts," she mused. Not all the years with Roger were bad, especially not the years when Robbie was a child. Perhaps it was the struggle of those early years, when her husband was just getting established in the automotive world, that had given their marriage a solid start.

"Roger! Why is that delivery truck pulling into our driveway?" Barbara asked as the truck backed expertly into the driveway.

"It's a surprise, Lovey. You and I are going to build a sauna in our basement."

"But our basement isn't even finished! We can't afford this."

"We can if we put it together ourselves. All we have to do is follow the directions. It will be easy."

It wasn't easy, Barb remembered, but it was fun. That's where she'd hang her chickadee. It would be a cheerful reminder of her trip each time she saw it outside the glass-etched sauna door.

She missed his sense of adventure and can-do attitude. He would never have allowed her to hang her chickadee outside the sauna, though, and she certainly did not miss his need to control her. She idly wondered how trophy wife Traci was handling that.

Her thoughts drifted to her son. Robbie resented his father's control, too, but he didn't have the patience to endure it as she did. He escaped into a world of drugs and lived on the edge of reality. Barb prayed daily that one day he would safely find his way into maturity and escape permanent harm.

"Linda?" she asked, turning to her companion. "Why do you do so many puzzles? Don't you get frustrated when you can't figure them out?"

Linda laughed. "No, I find working puzzles to be a good way to take my attention off the worries that clamor for my mind time. I guess I also want to delay memory loss as long as possible and I've heard that working puzzles keeps the brain healthy."

"I haven't thought about it that way," Barb replied. "I thought the goal was simply to fill in all the spaces correctly."

"No—that's the result, not the goal," Linda grinned. "It's the doing, not the getting, that is fun."

Barb thought about that as she combed her fingers through her blond hair, which was now showing a few streaks of gray. Perhaps that was the piece of life's puzzle she would take from this trip.

"Barb? Were you following Calendar Girls at all?" asked Linda.

"Yes, I hadn't seen it before today and, having spent time in England, I was interested to see the landscape and lifestyle again. Why do you ask?"

Linda shrugged out of her polar fleece jacket and folded it on her lap. "I've seen it once before and I had the same reaction this time. It seems like the story has two endings. The first story part gets resolved when the calendar gets published but then it sort of starts all over again when they start to deal with their success. "

"That seems to bother you," Barb observed.

"I guess I just wanted a happily-ever-after ending and then I had to worry that maybe it all wouldn't turn out after all."

Barb laughed. "So you like your entertainment plain and simple?"

"I guess so," Linda replied as she twisted the band around her long brown braid and tucked it behind her shoulder. "I worry enough about good endings in real life. Perhaps that's why I don't watch a lot of movies."

"I know one thing the movie did for me—it made me think about having a nice hot cup of brisk English tea," Barb responded. "I really developed a passion for tea during our stay in that country and I've come to appreciate its ability to settle me down."

Linda sighed. "Ah, yes—a cup of the Queen's Blend would do a lot to make me forget those orange barrels forming a parade outside the vacation bus window and impeding our progress to a nice, cozy, warm hotel."

Barb nodded in silent agreement. She couldn't do anything about happy endings any more than she could turn orange construction cones into candy corn. But she would have that cup of tea at the very first opportunity.

Settle Inn

T he luggage rack disappeared into the hotel lobby, with another following close behind. Evelyn looped her arm through Jackie's and helped her onto the curb. Negotiating different levels in the dark with a cane could be tricky and Jackie appreciated her friend's support. Emily handed them their room keycards as they passed through the lobby.

Jackie pointed out their room with her cane as they approached. "I am glad to be off that bus."

"Me, too," replied Evelyn as she slipped the keycard into the slot and turned the door handle.

"Oh, look, they turned the lights on for us," Jackie commented. "What a nice welcome."

Evelyn pulled their luggage inside and locked the door. "It is really nice to have an evening just to relax."

Jackie hung her cane on the door handle. She and her sister-in-law had taken several trips together since her brother's death several years earlier and they were compatible roommates. They had become best friends early in Evelyn's marriage to George and had shared many experiences over the years. In spite of the health care expenses during the last year of George's life, he had left

Evelyn a generous means of support and had encouraged her to travel with Jackie after his death.

"It's your turn to shower first tonight," Jackie said as she unzipped her suitcase and began shaking out her clothes.

Evelyn nodded. "Do you want me to go get some brochures from the lobby for you?" Jackie loved poring over the marketing materials so readily available at every stop.

"No, I picked up the Munising materials this morning when we left Sault Ste. Marie. But would you mind finding the weather station on the television for me? I need to plan what to wear tomorrow."

Evelyn smiled and clicked on the television to scroll through the channels.

"We have to decide what we are going to do tomorrow. I'll leave that decision for you to mull over while I'm in the shower," she commented.

Jackie fluffed up the pillow on the bed nearest the window and spread out the brochures on the paisley comforter. Munising offered a lot and they would have the entire day to explore, since they were staying tomorrow night, too. Waterfalls were enticing and the bus would be making the rounds of several of them, but she wasn't sure how far she would have to walk to actually see them. Since her hip surgery she had depended on her cane to keep her on her feet and preferred stable ground. The brochure stated that some of the waterfalls were handicap-accessible, however, so she didn't rule out the option completely.

The nature interpretation center at the National Lakeshore sounded interesting, too, but she knew Evie wouldn't be interested in a hike of any length. Her asthma plagued her after too long of a walk.

The Pictured Rocks Cruises were an obvious choice, but which one? A daytime cruise or the sunset cruise?

Those sandstone cliffs would look beautiful in the evening, but it might be too cool then. Jackie turned her attention to the weather girl and studied the radar screen. There were no green blotches to be seen—that was a good sign. The forecast was calling for a perfect day.

Jackie set aside the brochures and picked up the soft denim shirt she had hung over the back of the desk chair. Not too wrinkled, she thought, and the birdhouse design is repeated on the matching t-shirt so I can use the shirt as a light jacket if the breeze is sharp tomorrow. She grabbed a hanger from the closet and pulled the t-shirt out of her suitcase.

Evelyn popped her head out of the bathroom door.

"Do you need the iron? It's in here."

"I suppose that wouldn't hurt. I do like to start out the day as fresh as possible."

"The shower is all yours," Evelyn replied as she handed her the iron. "It's got a good strong flow, too."

"Thanks, Evie."

Evelyn toweled her hair dry and turned the channel, finally settling on a rerun of Andy Griffith. She enjoyed watching the black and white versions of old favorites and being reminded of simpler times.

This episode featured Aunt Bee suffering a social crisis. Evie recalled the storyline—Aunt Bee had won some big prizes on a quiz show and was showing them off to her friends. The inevitable jealousy soon became apparent to Aunt Bee.

Evelyn tucked herself into the cozy bed and closed her eyes. She had once thought that all her social problems would be over once she left high school. Nursing school didn't come with a set of friends, however, nor did she walk into a comfort circle in her first job at the Clintonville County Hospital.

The Griffiths were gathered in the living room discussing how Aunt Bee could solve the problem she had created for herself. The set reminded Evie of the living room in the house they had lived in when she was in high school. They didn't have Aunt Bee's kitchen, though. The fragrance of cinnamon and baked apples came to mind, as well as the many conversations she'd had with her mother as they worked together to prepare the family supper. She still missed her mother.

Given

"**E**velyn, get those potatoes peeled. I've got to get them boiling soon," her mother scolded.

"Mom, stop nagging—I'm working on it." Evelyn plopped another potato into the bowl of water and brushed the peelings into the gradually expanding pile of scraps. Helping her mother prepare supper for their family of six was not the highlight of her day but she preferred it over the clean-up chores afterward, which fell to a younger sister.

"Mom, remember I have play practice tonight."

"Don't you think you are pushing it a little hard? It seems like you are rarely home in the evenings these days and I'm worried your grades are going to slip."

"Well, Mom, I need time for school activities, too. You keep telling me if I want to go to college I have to get a scholarship—they don't give out scholarships on grades alone, and I'm never going to get there on my babysitting money."

Her mother sighed. She *was* concerned about Evie's involvement in so many things but the heart of it, she knew, was the knowledge that there were only two years left before her firstborn left home. The guilt of not being a stay-at-home Mom washed over her yet again. She knew she was bucking the tide with her unconventional decision but money was tight and they needed the extra income so their children could go to college.

Evelyn dumped the potato peelings in the pail to be emptied in the garden later. If she could just as easily dump the stress of the day, she thought; she'd bury it deep in that compost pile.

Thursday was usually her worst day of the week and today was no exception. Her first class of the day was also her most difficult. Geometry was incomprehensible to her on a good day but today it had been humiliating, as well. Tears came to her eyes as she placed the plates around the table.

"Evie, what's wrong?" her mother asked, handing her the silverware and turning back to the stove.

Evelyn slid onto a stool at the breakfast bar; telling her mother would likely result in yet another lecture about not studying enough, but not telling her would just prolong the pain. Her mother wouldn't let it go, she knew that.

"We had a pop quiz in Geometry this morning. There were only two problems but I didn't even know how to start solving them. The first step is always to write down 'given' and I didn't even do that. Mr. Shaney was in a really bad mood and didn't give us very much time. He said if we knew what we were doing, it wouldn't take us long."

"Did you do your homework last night?"

"I tried, but I just don't get it—I really did try. Anyway, Mr. Shaney looked at our papers and then he got into an even worse mood. I guess no one else got it, either. So he picked up my quiz and made fun because I didn't even write down 'given.' He called me "the girl who didn't get given." Of course, that's all I heard the rest of the day and everyone called me 'Givey' instead of 'Evie.'"

"Oh, Evie, remember that people only tease people they like."

"No, Mom, the kids that teased me weren't doing it for that reason. They were just being cruel."

Her mother silently turned the pork chops, knowing this emotional bruise would have to heal on its own.

"I think the teachers will all be in a better mood after the musical is over. Tonight is your second dress rehearsal, right? Saturday night it will be all over."

Evelyn retied the ribbon around her little sister's pony tail and pulled her up on her lap.

"We've put so much work into "Oklahoma!" I just hope everything goes well. Did you wash my black turtleneck? The stagehands have to wear all black so we can change the props and scenes without being spotted by the audience."

"It's hanging in the laundry room."

"Thanks. And did you remember that I need a ride to school on Saturday morning for the ACT test? I have to be there at 7 a.m. and it will be too dark to walk."

Her mother nodded, thinking that her daughter was not only growing up too fast for comfort, she was literally driving her every mile of the journey.

*

"Evelyn, hand me my hair dryer, would you please? This one doesn't work," Jackie called from the bathroom.

Evelyn reached into Jackie's overnight case and pulled out the blow dryer. Yes, she was very glad to have had such a faithful friend over the years. She would do anything for Jackie and she knew Jackie would stand by her, too.

*

"Mildred, check that waffle, I think it's smoking," Betty instructed.

The self-serve breakfast bar had a generous selection of choices and the waffle maker was very popular that morning. It only required pouring the pre-measured batter in plastic cups into the waffle iron, closing it and flipping it over until the timer dinged. But the timer on this machine had long since sounded its last chime and now it was a matter of estimating when the waffle was cooked.

"Yeah, yeah…I'm watching it. Go toast something while you wait your turn."

Emily strolled among the tables, clipboard in hand. Today's schedule offered the travelers several options, as did most days on the Dream Catcher Tour. She liked to keep track of what appealed to them so she could provide her employer with feedback to improve future tours.

"Ladies, may I have your attention, please?" she asked, positioning herself near the fireplace in the lounging area of the large room. "Raise your hand if you are planning to tour the area waterfalls today." Emily quickly counted the people in that group. "Sam will have the bus ready for you to board in an hour. Now, before I ask about the Pictured Rock cruises, please remember you have a choice tonight between the sunset cruise and the Summer Players dinner theater production of 'Arsenic and Old Lace.' If you are planning to do both, then take a daytime cruise. They depart every hour on the hour and the cruise takes 2 ½ to 3 hours. It's going to be a beautiful day for cruising."

Evie and Jackie quickly consulted. They had completely forgotten about the play. When Emily asked for a count of people taking a daytime cruise, their hands shot up.

"Lastly, how many are planning to hike one of the trails along Pictured Rocks National Lakeshore?" Emily was happy to see that Leslie and her Aunt Helen had raised their hands. "Sam will drop the hikers off at the park's interpretative center before proceeding with the waterfall tour, so meet the bus at 9:00 am, please. I will be going with the hikers, so if you have any questions or need assistance, please see Kirsten at the hotel desk. She is very knowledgeable about the area. Don't forget to wear your tour badge, as some places will give you a special discount if you are with a tour company."

Peace

An hour later a small group of hikers milled around in the interpretative center located at the trailhead. Emily walked up to Leslie, who was studying the trail map.

"Which hike are you and your aunt thinking of tackling?" she asked.

Leslie nodded to her aunt, who was huddled in front of a nature still-life display. "Well, it turns out that Aunt Helen has changed her mind about hiking."

Emily sat down on the pine bench and motioned for Leslie to join her; this might be her opportunity to spend more time with Leslie. "That's disappointing for you, I'm sure. Are you looking for a new hiking buddy? I was planning to just explore on my own but I'd love to have company."

"Oh, that would be great!" Leslie replied. "It's a lot more fun to hike with a buddy."

"What about Aunt Helen?"

The two of them sat in silence for a moment, watching Aunt Helen, who was now flanked by two young boys and a small girl with big blue eyes, staring gravely at a stuffed porcupine in the nature display. Helen kneeled and put her arm around the little girl's shoulder.

"Do you know how the porcupine got its quills?" She spoke solemnly to the child. The little girl slowly shook her head. Her brothers looked at each other and grinned—they sensed a story coming.

"It was a long, long time ago," Aunt Helen began. "They were called 'porcu's back then. And they had very curly hair shaped like circles all over their bodies. The porcus were teased by the other animals in the forest because of their hair. One day, a wood sprite came upon them and asked why they were so sad. They told her about their problem.

"And we can't even defend ourselves," they added. "Skunk can release a bad smell when he is scared. Fawn and her brother look just like the ground when Sun shines on their spots during their nap, so they are safe. And Cricket just stays very still on a blade of grass when he is afraid and no one sees him."

The wood sprite was a very clever creature. "What if I make your curls very, very straight AND make the tips very, very sharp?" she asked them. The porcus loved her idea.

"But how could she do that?" asked one of the boys, being drawn into the tale.

"The wood sprite had a plan. She was going to sew pine needles into their hair to make it straight and then breathe fairy dust on them to make them sharp. But first, she made the porcus promise something.

"Pine Tree is sharing her needles with you. You must promise always to remember the kindness she is showing to you today."

The porcus thought about that for a moment. "We can do that. From now on, we will no longer call ourselves porcus—we will be known as porcupines."

The two boys burst into giggles. Their little sister just continued to stare at the stuffed animal in the display case.

"I guess we don't have to worry about Aunt Helen entertaining herself while we hike," Emily laughed.

"No, she is quite capable of managing on her own. I am worried about her, though—she just seems so tired lately, and it's like her sense of adventure is diminished somehow. She tells me she feels fine but I know her too well to believe that."

"I know you are concerned. She is wisely staying within her limits and I think she'll talk to you when she's ready."

Leslie sighed. "A walk will do me good—how about taking the trail to Miner's Castle?"

Emily let Helen know which trail they were hiking and asked about her plans for the next two hours. Helen assured her she would be most content to find a comfortable spot outdoors to enjoy the view and catch up on the novel she had brought along.

The narrow trail wound through lush vegetation, with spectacular views of Lake Superior peeking through the trees. They walked in silence for several minutes, stopping frequently so Leslie could take pictures of the mushrooms and fungi that clearly thrived in this environment.

"You really seem to know what you are doing with that camera, Leslie."

"I love taking photographs. It's a hobby with a special meaning to me."

Emily gently held back the ferns to allow more sunlight to fall on the flower Leslie was considering.

"That's better—thank you. I was once told that light made the difference between a good picture and a great picture. Yesterday at Tahquamenon Falls I got a really good picture of a small creek spilling down a hill and the brief bit of sunlight streaming through the trees gave it this mottled green look with these acorn brown/butternut highlights on the surface. I am sure that one will be a beautiful print. "

"You said that photography was a hobby with a special meaning to you—do you mind telling me why?"

Leslie straightened up and looked at Emily. She retied the sweater around her waist and started back down the trail, making room for Emily to walk next to her instead of single file.

"It's a long story," she warned. "And it doesn't have a happy ending."

"Oh, I don't mean to press you. I am just interested in learning how things become special to people."

"It's okay. I haven't talked about this for a long time and seeing this undergrowth and beautiful foliage must have triggered a little nostalgia."

Emily adjusted her stride to match Leslie's. She was several inches taller than Leslie and she didn't want her long legs to get ahead of Leslie's story.

"His name was Steve. We met in college and I was attracted to his intensity in everything he did—he seemed to have boundless energy and an interest in so many things. But it wasn't all about him—he had a heart that reached out to those who hadn't been born privileged, as he had been. Naturally, I fell in love with him."

"Naturally—it is fun to be around people who are fun," Emily responded.

"Oh, Steve was great fun. But he could be serious, too. He was majoring in film and media and once a professor told him that his photographs lacked integrity. Steve agonized over that comment for the longest time, but it did motivate him to really learn the mechanics of photography and not rely too heavily on his creativity."

Emily stopped so Leslie could negotiate the steep trail ahead. They were steadily climbing and some of the transitions were rather abrupt. When the trail widened again Emily picked up the conversation.

"I used to believe that people stopped doing things they enjoyed or were good at because other things crowded them out and there just wasn't time for everything. Or that dreams died because people simply gave up on them. Now I think that dreams die a little at a time, and that most of them don't die of natural causes. Each unkind word of thoughtless criticism, each word of support unspoken gradually drains the life out of them until they are just empty shells. Steve didn't give up on photography, did he?"

"No. It discouraged him for a while but photography wasn't his passion."

The two women stepped aside and allowed a family of four to hike past them.

"His passion was helping people," Leslie continued. "When the Peace Corp recruiters came to our campus he knew he'd found his calling for the next two years of his life."

"What about your relationship? Long distance romances are so difficult." Emily spoke from bitter experience.

Leslie turned to smile at Emily. "Oh, it wasn't long distance—I married him and went with him."

Emily stepped off the trail and found a fallen log to sit on. She wasn't hiking another step until she heard the rest of this story.

"Where did you go?"

"Guatemala—hot, steamy, with jungle roads that were incredibly steep. We were assigned to several wide-spread villages and Steve's job was to work with the youth groups. I remember how excited Steve was about his first project. He was going to teach the kids how to make papier-mâché puppets and use them to create little skits that represented both their culture and ours. He hauled all the supplies up there—old paper, buckets, a sack of flour—and then no one showed up for the youth group event. He was so disappointed.

"That night the monsoons started and the shack we lived in offered about as much protection as Mary Poppins' umbrella. It was cold and as we huddled together under the thin blankets I wished with all my heart that we could go back home to Boston."

Emily brushed a stray hair behind her ear while taking a long sip from her water bottle.

"How long was your assignment?" she asked.

"The Peace Corp commitment is for two years plus three months' training. It didn't seem very long when we signed up and, while our parents were not happy with us for rushing into marriage so young, they did support us."

"Did it seem like forever?"

"We gradually adjusted and Steve was enthusiastic about immersing himself in the culture and learning all he could about the people. I worked at a medical clinic in a nearby village while he continued to work with the youth. He took numerous pictures because one of the goals of the Peace Corp is to promote understanding about other countries and cultures when you return home. He dreamed about the presentations he would give and had decided to change his major to education and go into teaching.

About six months after we arrived, he scheduled a talent show for several of his groups. He was so thrilled when the youth from the remote village actually came down in an old bus, bringing the puppets they eventually created. They even made them dance to the mariachi band that another youth group had formed. It was the best night of his volunteer experience and he couldn't stop talking about it afterwards. It seemed to be a turning point for him and after that he kept jumping up out of bed to grab his notebook and jot down more ideas.

The next day I rode my bike to the clinic in the village. I was unloading a shipment of medical supplies and recording the inventory when the doctor found me. He ushered me into his tiny office and told me I'd best sit down. I was suddenly overwhelmed by a sense of enormous loss and I knew that somehow my life had just changed forever. The doctor told me that Steve had been found lying on the floor of the garage they had used for the talent show. He had suffered a fatal brain aneurysm."

Emily stared at her. "I cannot imagine your heartbreak—I am so sorry."

"I was only 21 years old and it felt like my life had ended, too. The Peace Corp released me from my commitment and I went back home to finish college. But it turns out Steve really was the love of my life and I never completely recovered from losing him—he was my greatest adventure."

"Did you ever marry again, may I ask?" Emily asked.

"No. After college I gradually became absorbed in a career with a large non-profit organization and then my parents were killed in a private plane crash. Aunt Helen encouraged me to take over their business. My parents were antique dealers and traveled a lot. I think she thought it would help me stay connected to them somehow. But that business was their dream, not mine. She took me under her wing then and has been my dear mentor and friend ever since."

Emily stood up. "I understand now why you are so sensitive to Aunt Helen's unusual behavior lately—you've suffered such critical losses in your life."

"I didn't realize it, but I think you are right. She has been my anchor for so many years now." She brushed the twigs from her walking shorts and stepped back onto the trail. "When I lost Steve I worried that I would forget him too soon. I was so young and I did expect that I would marry again and have a family. I do a lot of analysis in my job and I look for trends in the data and create timelines and charts for this reason or that. A chart of my life would show a huge spike during my college years and then a fairly steady line after that. I think most women expect the peak of their lives to come a little later in life than mine did."

Emily thought about that as they hiked in companionable silence. She guessed that a chart of her life would show a series of points going up and down but within a relatively narrow range. She could name the highlights and the low points easily enough but couldn't think of anything that she would consider an off-the-chart spike. Maybe she was one of those people who peaked later in life.

"But I didn't have to worry about forgetting Steve," Leslie continued. "He and his Aunt Helen - now my adopted Aunt Helen - shared the same the mischievous eyes which they laughingly described as 'pond-scum green' inherited from special Irish elves."

Emily laughed and glanced at the Lake Superior shore playing hide and seek through the tree line. Life certainly had been a journey through deep shadows for her new friend.

Side Trip

S am turned into the Lakenenland Sculpture Park
parking lot, east of Marquette. He couldn't believe he
had let Emily talk him into this little side trip.

"But, Sam, it's unique and we have plenty of time. We
don't have to be in L'Anse until early evening and we have
dinner reservations in Michigamme. The women will love
it."

A glance out the window quickly confirmed Sam's
suspicions. He would need his best sheepdog tricks to
round the women up after they scattered among these
sculptures. Karen was already heading towards a metal
praying mantis perched on an old tree stump. He sincerely
hoped that none of the sculptures were for sale.

"Oh, that's spectacular!" Lynn exclaimed, kneeling
next to a six-foot alligator sprawled across a woodchip bed.
All the sculptures in this park were made of metal and most
were on a large scale. Some were whimsical, some
decidedly cute, and a few represented the logging history of
the area, such as the one of two men frozen in the act of
working the two-man saw.

"I love the wolf on the buggy," Jean said. "The wheels
are made of circular saws."

Betty snapped a photo of the star-gazer while Terry ran delightedly from exhibit to exhibit. Emily grinned at Sam, who was seated next to her on the park bench.

"I can't resist it—I told you so."

"I don't see a golfer sculpture," he shot back.

"I'm sure there is one somewhere but you won't find it sitting here."

Sam got up and stood on the bench.

"What are you doing, Sam?"

"I'm looking for Jackie. It's easy to get a cane tripped up on this kind of ground. There are a lot of hidden rocks and unexpected crevices."

Emily grinned. Sam talked tough but he had a soft spot for his passengers that he tried to conceal from her.

"Let's start rounding them up—it will take a good fifteen minutes to get everyone back on the bus," she said. "I'll remind them that Jilbert's Dairy is our next stop, that will lure them."

Your Purse Is Ringing

"Donna, your purse is ringing," Louise said to her friend, who was shuffling packages in the overhead bin to make room for one more gift bag.

"Thanks. The phone is in the side pocket. Would you mind handing it to me?"

Donna flipped open the phone and cradled it on her shoulder.

"Yes, honey, I can hear you. Yes, I know, but sometimes there's no reception up here. Sweetie, how about if you tell Grammy that when I get home? Put your mommy on, okay?"

Donna settled back into her seat and leaned closer to the window, hoping to improve the reception.

"Kristen, I hear you. But she's going to be your sister in-law in another three months, whether you like her or not. You're not going to change her. You need to cooperate for your brother's sake.

"I know, Kristen. I know puff sleeves aren't flattering. Your arms will not look like toothpicks stuck into a peach mushroom. Just go with it—the dresses have been ordered."

Louise chuckled. She had built quite an image of the anticipated wedding of her best friend's son and was looking forward to attending the event in October. She sympathized with Donna's dilemma in trying to appease both of her children. The bride-to-be was certainly living up to the maniac bride stereotype.

"Kristen, she's a vegetarian. She can serve whatever she wants at the wedding dinner. I'm sure there will be some meat entrees. Your brother will insist on it. Try not to worry about it."

Donna closed the phone and slipped it into her shirt pocket, a pocket she had designed just for that purpose. Donna loved to sew and preferred to make most of her own clothes. She loved tweaking patterns to accommodate her conveniences and adjust the comfort level to adapt to the shape-shifting that seemed to come as part of the aging package.

"Louise, I am so grateful to you for going on this trip with me—I really needed to get away from all that wedding hoopla."

"Maybe it's just the wedding planning that is causing her to be such a pain. Perhaps she'll settle down after she's married."

"I'd love to go with that theory, Louise, but she's a control freak and insists on her way or no way. I can't imagine what my son sees in her, but he picked her—I just have to work with it as best I can."

"I admire you for your attitude, Donna. I don't think I could be as diplomatic as I've seen you be with the whole situation."

"I try to pick my battles with her and not get drawn into every argument. I did insist on being able to wear comfortable shoes to the wedding, for example. I can't believe she thought I would be able to walk in spiked heels—she's the slave to fashion, not me."

Louise laughed at the mental image of Donna mincing down the aisle in high heels with pointy toes. Someday the bride would learn about age-appropriate attire, but in the meantime, she looked forward to the fashion show the wedding plans seemed to promise.

Double Dip

I vy and Carol were born on the same day of the same month, two years apart.. Although separated by age, nothing could separate the bond between them. In everything else, however, they were divided. At the moment, they were arguing about cows.

"It's a Holstein, Carol," Ivy insisted.

"No, you're wrong—it's one of those Guernsey-types, I think." Carol always thought she was right, but Ivy knew she was actually the one who got things straight—at least, that is what *she* thought. Carol would always argue, of course.

The object of contention was perched atop a huge milk tank. They had just pulled into the parking lot of Jilbert's Dairy in Marquette. Emily knew that Jilly was a Holstein but she wisely stepped aside, avoiding both the discussion at hand and the sisters as they descended the stairs of the bus. Her focus was locked in on which topping she would select for the delicious treat she was soon to enjoy.

"Well, ice cream is made from milk and milk comes from Guernseys," Carol continued.

Ivy sighed. "Carol, there are black and white spots all over the cow. There's only one kind of cow that has spots and that's a Holstein."

Jilbert's was more than an ice cream stop on a hot August day in the Upper Peninsula; it had become a dairy museum as well as a milk processing plant, and antique milk bottles and vintage dairy advertising were to be enjoyed as much as the ice cream.

"Divide and conquer time," announced Emily as the women gathered under the black-and-white spotted awnings shading the entrance. "They can't serve us all at once. The collections of dairy memorabilia begin to the left of the entrance. Follow those to the viewing windows, where you can see the processing plant in action. The serving counter is to the right and the country store is in back. Don't worry—they won't run out of ice cream."

Ivy and Carol stood in front of the viewing window, noses pressed against the glass like school children. Ivy nudged Carol aside so she could get a better vantage point. Carol didn't even notice. Being both smaller and younger than her sister, she had long ago learned to move aside.

"Remember when the milk came in little bottles, when we were kids?" Ivy asked.

"Oh, Ivy, we're not that old—school milk has always been in cartons," Carol replied. "You just dress old."

"No, I remember the milk crates and the cellophane tops on the bottles with the paper band. We used to wrap the bands around our ring fingers and pretend we were engaged. And I don't dress 'old'. I always select age-appropriate styles."

"If that shapeless blouse suits you, then maybe you are old," Carol shot back. "I think you're crazy—you're probably remembering a story Mom told."

As with most of their bickering, there was no resolution. They moved on down the hallway.

"Look at the storage room," Carol said as she passed an open doorway. "It's so organized and neat."

86

"Now what you are you implying?" Ivy responded. "Just because you are a neat freak is no reason to constantly harp on me."

"Well, we did have to put masking tape down the middle of our room when we were kids so I could prove to Dad that I kept my side clean." Their father had craved peace and their mother would often sigh and announce that she could live like a queen if her girls didn't fight. Carol smiled as the memory fluttered across her mind.

"Oh, you are just too fussy—loosen up and live a little." Ivy never concerned herself with the minor details of life; that was Carol's responsibility.

The sisters walked back to the front of the store and stopped in front of the ice cream case.

"Oh, my goodness, there are way too many choices," Ivy wailed. "How am I ever going to decide?"

"Don't be ridiculous," Carol replied. "You always get chocolate, I always get vanilla. You always get a double dip, I always get a single dip. That's the way life is. Don't tip the canoe."

Ivy turned her back on her sister and flip-flopped her way to the counter. "A double-dip chocolate, please." Once in a blue moon ice cream world, her sister was right.

Sam took his Moose Tracks triple dip cone and stepped out of the way of the two women to find a patch of peace far away from them.

*

Emily flipped on the microphone and waited for the women to give her their attention.

"Ladies, Sam is going to stop at the shopping center, where there's a large discount superstore. Many of you have requested a chance to pick up a few things to refill your travel supplies—you only have a half an hour, so start thinking about what you need. We want to get to Michigamme on time for our dinner reservation."

An hour and a half hour later Emily moved slowly down the aisle, passing the bag of chocolate kisses to her traveling guests.

"What's the problem?" asked Jean. "We aren't moving very fast."

"There's an accident ahead and it's causing quite a back-up. Since we are on a highway and not a freeway, there's no way to get around it. I've called ahead to the restaurant and told them we are being delayed."

"Thanks, and thanks for the treats. A couple of kisses will take the edge off my appetite. Tell Sam we want him to install a coffee machine on the bus," smiled Jean.

"And tell Terry that singing 'Rollin', Rollin', Rollin'' isn't going to speed things along, either," Betty chimed in.

Marianne tucked the silver candy wrappers into her pocket and pulled out a slim pen. Opening the small spiral-bound notebook to a blank page, she wrote down the date and place where she had made her latest purchases. A lifetime of frugality had fostered a need to account for every dime she spent. She loved the habit—it maintained a reassuring sense of order in her life that made her feel comfortable.

She had carefully planned her souvenir purchases during this trip. The trips they had taken while their children were growing up had been limited to visiting family. There had been the occasional day trip but her husband saw family destination vacations as expensive, unnecessary and an interference with his work. This solo vacation, her first, was going to include tangible reminders to savor in the years to come.

She had originally planned to follow her grandmother's example and collect a few Christmas ornaments that would serve in the years ahead as reminders of this special time. But as she experienced the nuances of each day on tour with the other women, she realized she needed something else, something that would remind her in a more personal way of each friend she had made. It hadn't taken her long to realize that it would be people, not places, who were to make the trip memorable for her.

During the early days of the trip her companions had all seemed much the same, but with each passing day she had come to see the uniqueness of each woman. Cookie cutters came to mind; tools that cut each shape identically in the dough and kept it that way until the dough began to bake. Heat was responsible for the first subtle differences and cooling and decorating completed the transformation. No two cookies in the batch came out alike. Although they shared many similarities, she was also certain that no two women on the trip were the same.

Marianne neatly wrote 'teddy bears' on the page and made a note that the set of three was $6.95 plus tax.

In the seat beside her, Terry thumbed through the cookbook.

"Terry, do you bake much?" asked Marianne. "I love to bake."

"Me? No, I don't have much luck with baking. I don't have the patience. You have to bake a lot to really get good at it."

"I notice you picking up cookbooks, though," Marianne responded. "What do you like to cook?"

"I guess I just like to read cookbooks. And collect things." Terry smiled. Sam had again reprimanded her for the growing pile of bags with her name on them in the cargo hold. If he only knew that sometimes the purchases never came out of their bags. Sam would not understand the compulsions that drove a shopaholic.

"You must have a big house, then."

Terry laughed merrily. "No, but I do use every bit of the space I have."

Marianne idly wondered if Terry's house had the same free-flowing flair that her clothing expressed. It would be fun to decorate the Terry cookies, she thought.

Sam pulled the last of the luggage from the hold and put it on the rolling rack the motel had provided. It was a relief to finally be in L'Anse, their anchor point for the exploration of the Keweenaw Peninsula, and he was looking forward to the two-night stay.

House Dressing

T he cool Michigan morning splashed into view as they stepped out of the shadows of the motel. Marilyn loved easing into the day with her traveling companions. The roadside restaurants provided hearty portions of delicious food and the fresh air sharpened not only her appetite but all of her senses, too. The fragrant pine smell was replaced by the aroma of freshly roasted coffee as they entered the large dining room.

Settling around a table near the picture window, the three women with Marilyn picked up the menus and began the difficult selection process.

"This fresh air certainly perks up my appetite," Jody laughed. "Shall I have the Blue Ox Breakfast Special or go for the Lumberjack Lite?

Linda chuckled as she turned the menu page. "A Lumberjack Lite could probably feed this whole table."

Marilyn already knew she was going to order the blueberry pancakes, so she turned her attention to the décor. Decorating was her passion. At first glance, the Birch View Restaurant would feed Marilyn's enthusiasm for her hobby as well as her stomach.

Knotty pine panels lined the walls and several wooden shelves held a wide variety of Upper Peninsula collectibles. Scenes painted on saw blades and old pails, three-dimensional needle art, and a smattering of fired pottery and ceramic pieces were interspersed with antique tools-turned-art. Marilyn pulled out her camera phone and snapped a picture of the centerpiece on their table: a small brass lantern holding a fern and a few small daisies. Through the glass sides of the lantern, the artful arrangement appeared to be underwater. She pictured the perfect spot for such an accent piece in her home—now all she had to do was find the little brass lantern. Switching on the voice memo feature of her phone, she quickly described an idea of how she might fill the centerpiece.

"...and that'll do it," Emily finished. Marilyn suddenly realized it was her turn to order. "Blueberry pancakes, please. Do you have any special brews of coffee going this morning?"

"Actually, we do," replied the young server. "Lighthouse Blend is truly awesome."

"I love trying flavored coffees," Marilyn shared. "I'll have that, too."

"Okay, ladies, fess up—what's going to be on your plates this morning? I wasn't paying attention when you ordered," Marilyn questioned. Her three companions simply smiled.

"Do you work for a library or a museum, Marilyn?" Jody inquired. "I see you documenting everything you see on this trip. What are you going to do with all that information you're gathering?"

"Oh, I wish I had that kind of experience to draw on, but my jobs have been much more chaotic than that. My work has always been in customer service. No, I document everything for a different reason—what do you think it is?"

Jody spoke up first. "I think you just love playing with the technology. You change your ring tone every few days."

"No, I think it's because you see everything through your decorator eyes and secretly want to audition for one of those make-over cable shows," said Linda.

Emily grinned at their suggestions but didn't offer her opinion.

"Oh, my goodness!" exclaimed Marilyn as their food arrived. "You ordered the giant cinnamon rolls!" The sweet treats were famous in the Upper Peninsula both for their size and taste. "They are as big as dinner plates."

"They are five inches in diameter and three inches high," announced Linda. "And dripping in glaze, too, I might add."

Emily rolled her eyes at them both. "You aren't going to make me deal with a sugar crash today, are you?"

"Don't worry, Emily, we can handle our sugar." They inched their chairs back another fraction to ensure they had enough stomach space.

Marilyn tipped the bottle to drizzle maple syrup across her Made in Michigan breakfast, both of which, according to the menu description, were products of the U.P.

Jody swallowed a mouthful and returned to the conversation. "Now tell us, Marilyn—why do you document everything?"

Emily caught a sudden shadow darkening the gold flecks in Marilyn's warm brown eyes. Laying her fork next to her plate, she gave her full attention to the exchange.

"Well, don't laugh, please," Marilyn began. "I document everything because I just can't remember things like I once did. I used to be teased for having a photographic memory and now I need a real camera to remember the details for me."

"Oh, that's a normal part of aging," Linda reassured her. "We all forget things more often than we used to."

"I know that, but I'm beginning to think this is more than natural forgetfulness—it's like the picture frame is still on the wall but the picture is missing. I know I knew something at one time but I can't bring to mind the name for it or quite remember what it is that I'm missing. The placeholder is in my brain but not the object I'm trying to remember."

Jody was thoughtful for a moment, her sweet roll temporarily forgotten. "I think the time to begin worrying is when you don't know that you've forgotten something. If it's just out of reach it is still in normal range of memory, at least at our age."

Emily rested her elbows on the table and leaned forward. "Why don't you talk to Jean about this, Marilyn? I heard her talking to Betty about her mother-in-law's battle with Alzheimer's. I'm sure she would be willing to share what she has learned."

"Thank you. It does help to talk about this. I think I'm getting a little obsessed about it," Marilyn replied.

Emily sat back and chewed on the conversation while the women polished off the last few bites of their breakfasts. This was another aspect of aging that Emily feared, even though she had no reason to yet. She lived by her wits—how would she support herself if her brain cells started taking permanent vacations?

Sam had the bus pulled up and ready for boarding. Emily stood by with her clipboard, checking off each name as Sam provided assistance as needed. The routine was well established now and boarding went smoothly, especially since no shopping had yet occurred.

"We have a beautiful day to explore this wonderful part of the Upper Peninsula," Emily spoke into the microphone. "I'd like to introduce to our step-on guide for today. This is Bill Campbell, a high school teacher at Calumet High

School. He will be traveling with us today to explain the rich history and culture of the Keweenaw area. We will make a few stay-on-the-bus stops at points of interest along the way and he will share with us some of the history of Calumet. There is also a walking tour of Calumet that you may choose if you prefer not to go to Copper Harbor this afternoon. We will spend some time at Fort Wilkins State Park, which features living history programs, in addition to exploring Copper Harbor itself. At five o'clock Sam will pick up the people who stay in Calumet and then we'll go to Houghton, where we have dinner reservations tonight at the Northern Lights Restaurant. Plan your lunch and snacks accordingly," she concluded, giving the cinnamon roll ladies a sharp look.

Italian Hall

Stepping out of the shadow of the bus, Madeline Harris edged her way to the front of the group. The step-on guide stood near the tall archway in the center of the small lot, which was identified as the Italian Hall Memorial Park.

The guide removed his cap and folded his hands as he spoke. "It was Christmas Eve, 1913, and the miners had been on strike for five months. A yuletide party had been organized for the families of the striking miners at the Italian Hall that once stood on this site. At the peak of the party, someone yelled 'FIRE!'' and panic ensued. Seventy-three people, over half of them children, died in their attempt to escape the impending tragedy—the real tragedy, however, was that there was no fire."

Madeline stared at the unkempt lot as the guide continued. "They say the party was organized by Big Annie Clement, a tall woman who became identified as the heart and soul of the miners' cause. She and Mother Jones, who was an 83-year-old labor activist, rallied the women and children to the support of the miners. Many Calumet businesses had withdrawn strikers' credit privileges and the union, the Western Federation of Miners, never made good on its promise of strike relief pay." As was common to natives of the Upper Peninsula, the guide used words sparsely, leaving his listeners to piece together the story between the lines he spoke.

"How many people attended the party?" asked one of the women.

"The party was in the second-floor ballroom of the hall and there were almost seven hundred people, so even though a union card was required for identification, it became impossible to account for everyone."

"Why would someone yell fire if there was no fire?" puzzled Terry.

"It's a mystery to this day. Remember, strike breakers had been brought in and it was a very tense time for these people. Many believe the call was intentional. Some say the man was wearing a white Citizens' Alliance button, a sign of a strike breaker. Some think there were two men who shouted the panic word. Others believe that it was a drunken prank gone bad. No one knows for sure."

"I don't understand. Why couldn't they get out?" Jean asked.

The guide looked at the group and pointed up to the arch. "The doors had an odd design—there were two sets: one set opening outward toward the street, the second set opening inward to the stairwell. The running children piled up against the closed inner doors, and with the crush behind them, no one could get them opened. Most of the deaths were due to suffocation. Now there are laws that forbid the design of doors opening inward."

"Thank you, Mr. Campbell," Emily said as she shook his hand. "We really appreciate your history lesson and the fact that this memorial to such a tragedy is not forgotten."

The woman silently filed back onto the bus. Emily turned to see Madeline kneeling near the arch, quietly pulling weeds and brushing dirt from the brick pathway. "Come, Maddie, we have to move on."

Madeline got back on the bus, but in her heart and mind she knew she could not move on just yet. Settling into her seat, she looked at the schedule for the day and remembered that the afternoon included an optional side trip to Copper Harbor or free time in historic Calumet. Turning to her friends, she informed them that she would be taking the free time instead of the side trip.

"Why, Maddie?" asked Maggie. "I thought you wanted to stock up on thimbleberry jam."

"Perhaps you could pick some up for me. I'm going to find a library or museum or something and do some more research on the Italian Hall tragedy. This will make a fantastic Social Studies unit for my eighth graders next year. I've been looking for a subject that would intrigue them into learning some of the required Michigan standards objectives and I think I've hit the mother lode with this topic. I can't wait to get started on my unit plan."

Maggie laughed. "So you're going to turn into Mrs. Harris for the afternoon and just abandon us?"

"You bet," Madeline replied. "You know I can't pass up planning a teachable moment."

*

Madeline swallowed the last bite of her pasty and threw the wrapper into the trash can near the entrance to the City Hall. She was so glad that she was able to get pasties in her suburban Metro Detroit community, although they weren't quite as good as the one she had just enjoyed. They were the perfect lunch box entrée.

The hot summer day held a slight breeze and Maddie intended to take full advantage of it. She headed to a table

near an open window. The third floor of the old hall, filled
with books that had made comfortable homes of the shelves
for many decades, seemed to welcome her presence.

As was her habit when settling into a planning session,
Maddie pushed her glasses to the top of her head and
pictured herself in her favorite teaching outfit: a black
jumper, white blouse, sensible shoes, and a splash of large
jewelry around her neck. She was Mrs. Harris now.

Next, she pictured her students. It took her a moment to
get past their attire. The fashion trends of the past year
made most of them look like walking magnets for found
objects. If it didn't fit, was supposed to be worn underneath
instead of on top, and had sleeves and pant legs totally out
of proportion to limb size, it was mainstream for them.
Thankfully, a dress code was in place for the new school
year.

After thirty-five years in the classroom, she knew the
bell curve would likely hold true for this year's class; she
would be challenged by a few who preferred extreme
behavior but the majority would settle into a predicable
learning routine. Her job was to break up the predictability
and engage their interest to gain entrance to their minds.
Then she could introduce new ideas and different
perspectives and encourage them to grow.

She began by drawing a grid on a page in her spiral
notebook and titling it "Italian Hall." Labeling each square
with a curriculum heading, she quickly sorted her initial
ideas into the appropriate boxes. Investigating mining
practices of the early 1900s and the widow-maker were
penciled in under science. Staring at the street outside the
window, an art lesson began to take shape: abstracts using
geometric shapes that suggested townscapes. She knew the
cultural scene of Calumet in those days attracted famous
performers and high society had found a solid footing this

far north. That would inspire lessons for music and language arts.

After another hour of reading old mining journals and an anthology of *The Daily Mining Gazette*, her planning grid was crowded with ideas. For the inevitable drama queen, she pictured a re-enactment of a funeral for a young miner where a selected girl would dress in bridal attire to symbolize the future that was lost with the man's untimely death. In order to balance the serious topics they would explore, she envisioned a fantasy baseball tournament between the workers of the various mines.

But the centerpiece of the unit would have to be the escalating tensions between the union and the company, for that is what cast the cruel shadow over the tragedy memorialized in the small park. Her students would instinctively share the catastrophic sense of loss, as they would have been the same average age as the children lost in Italian Hall when they experienced 9/11.

She would have to separate fact from emotion and give full measure to each. Perhaps a debate could serve to represent both sides of the issue. That approach would serve to develop teamwork and focus the students on solid research and crafting firm arguments for each viewpoint. A news program format always worked well for her and would allow for expression of the towns people who were caught between the miners and the mining company dispute and also provide a forum for the debate. It would give a voice to Annie Clement, too.

Now for the emotional side: how could she touch on the nerves that vibrated nearly a century ago in this small, diverse community and make common connections to the situations today's kids had already experienced and would face in the future? And which nerves? Her students were just now crossing that ever-moving line between childhood and adolescence. She slumped back in her chair and let her glasses dangle on the chain that kept them in constant reach. The gap between then and now seemed greater than what could be measured in mere years. Yet, she knew it could be crossed—the common denominators were clear to her.

She had to approach it from the students' world and work backwards. That meant making the connection through cyberspace—not exactly her comfort zone, but Madeline knew she could coerce her son into setting up a website and securing it for a classroom blog space. She would call it MyOldSpace.com and have the students make their journal entries from the perspective of the kids of Calumet in 1913. They would be allowed to write about whatever personal feelings they chose, as long as their thoughts were expressed within the framework of that tumultuous time at the height of copper mining. She supposed her ground rules would have to disallow instant messaging shorthand, but she would encourage them to invent the equivalent of instant messaging that their peers of long ago surely would have created; kids have always communicated in code.

Maddie glanced at her Mickey Mouse watch. She had another half hour before meeting the bus but the humid air and quiet surrounds were making her sleepy. Returning the materials she had been using to the librarian's desk, she found her way to the park bench she had noticed under the shady maple tree outside the window. Just enough time for a refreshing little nap, she thought. She set the alarm on her cell phone for 20 minutes, tucked it in an outside pocket of her briefcase purse, and leaned back on the sun-warmed bench. As the soft breeze massaged her eyes and to the sound of bees buzzing nearby, she nodded off to a gentle sleep.

*

December 24, 1913. Christmas Eve day is finally here. I am so glad to have a happy day to enjoy. We need some happy time. I have a lot to do today so I'll have to write more tonight.

Cora tied the leather cord around her diary and slipped it into her dresser drawer.

"I'm coming, Ma," she shouted as she pulled her cloak and bonnet from the wardrobe.

"Cora, you must have breakfast. I know you are excited but sit down first and have your oatmeal," her mother ordered.

Cora reached for the honey and a piece of toast. She thought, as she always did, of the wealth on her table at mealtime and the tables of those whose bowls were empty. These included the bowl of her best friend Brida—a friend she was now forbidden to see outside of school because of the miner's strike. Cora hated the strike but she understood why Brida's father had chosen to support it. She couldn't imagine life without her own father, and worried with Brida about the danger Brida's father faced each time he rode the rail down into the mine.

"Cora, you're hogging the honey," her little brother said. "Save some for me."

Cora glanced at him then silently passed the honey. Ditching him today was going to be a problem. Her mother would certainly expect her to keep him busy while she finished her Christmas preparations.

Her mother set a covered basket with a ribbon tied gaily around the handle on the sideboard. "Don't forget to take this basket of baked bread to Mrs. Higgins when you go to your piano rehearsal this morning," she reminded Cora.

Goodness, she'd completely forgotten the piano appointment. They were going to go over her music one more time before tonight's Christmas Eve Children's Service. Cora was the accompanist for the Sunday school and while she certainly hadn't forgotten that, she had forgotten about the extra rehearsal. This may be my opportunity to see Brida, she thought. Her little brother never accompanied her to see Mrs. Higgins.

Grabbing the basket, she headed to the front hall. Her mother followed her.

"Cora, listen to me—be very careful. The tensions in this town won't take a holiday break. Pay attention to your surroundings and don't daydream."

Cora nodded. She knew the warning by heart. Her family was neither miner nor mining company, but in that difficult middle ground of merchant. Her father owned the Great Atlantic and Pacific Tea Company commonly known as the A&P and, despite the pressure, had not joined the Citizen's Alliance or any support group for either side of the current confrontation. Cora knew how difficult it was for him to try to stay neutral in this polarized town.

Mrs. Higgins cracked open the door. "Oh, it's you, Cora. Come in."

"Weren't you expecting me?"

"Of course, my dear, but you can't be too careful these days."

Cora handed her the basket and untied her bonnet. Following Mrs. Higgins into the small parlor, she thought once again that this Christmas would see no peace.

The cold wind blasted her face as she turned the corner and headed to her father's store. She purposely walked an extra block and circled back so she could pass the entrance of the Italian Hall before arriving at the A&P, which occupied the ground floor on the other end of the huge building. Brida was planning to help the women get the hall ready for the big party planned for that evening, and if her plan was successful she would drop a red mitten as a sign for Cora.

Cora spotted the splotch of red in the corner near the back of the steps. She picked it up, shook off the snow and looked around before casually walking into the hall entryway. She dared not go any further lest she draw attention to herself. She knew Brida would be watching for her.

"Cora! You made it." Brida ran down the stairs, her white-blond braids flying, and gave Cora a big hug. "I was so hoping I could wish you a Merry Christmas today."

"I know. It seems like it has been more than a week since school ended for the holidays. I really miss you," Cora replied. "I can't stay, of course, but at least we got to see each other today."

"Yes, that was one of my many Christmas wishes," Brida told her. "The party is going to be so great. The ballroom on the second floor is decorated and lots and lots of presents have been donated and the Mother Goose play is going to be so much fun. Miss Annie worked really, really hard to organize all of this for us." Brida was breathless with excitement.

The big doors swung open and the girls slipped into the corner as a huge evergreen tree was dragged through the entrance and up the stairs.

"I've got to go," Brida whispered.

"Me, too—Pa is expecting me at the store."

"Merry Christmas!" they said to each other in unison.

A gentle snow fell softly as Cora and her brother hurried through the side door and down the narrow stairs of the National Lutheran Church that evening. The church was only a block away from the Italian Hall and Cora put the thought of her school friends gathering for their grand party out of her mind. She was getting very nervous about her own responsibility that evening.

Cora smoothed the peach ruffles on her dress and sat down on the piano bench. She felt the cool air steal around her ankles as she checked her music one more time, folded her hands in her lap, and waited for the signal to begin the procession. Hearing the excited yet muffled chatter rising from the basement, she could have played 'Three Blind Mice' for all the children would notice. The thought made her smile and relax.

An hour later, the last chorus of 'Joy to the World' faded into the night and the children filed two by two down the aisle to the basement to await their parents and get their Christmas gifts.

Cora was the last to leave the church, but instead of following the others downstairs, she took advantage of the excited chaos to slip outside. Hugging her arms around herself to ward off the cold, she thought briefly of her friends and the fun they were having.

"Cora! There you are," her father called. "Come aside, I must talk to you."

"What is wrong, Papa? Why aren't you smiling?"

"Something terrible has happened, Cora. We must sit down." Cora followed him back into the church and sat beside him in the back pew.

Dear Diary, I am writing by the flicker of a candle and can barely see what I am writing through this wall of tears. The most evil, horrible event I could never have imagined has ripped my heart apart. Tonight, while we were singing Christmas into life, other children, only a block away, were screaming their last breaths. I can only be thankful that Brida survived the panic. Her little sister, and over seventy other people, most of them children, did not—all because a

*man shouted "fire" when he knew there was no fire. How
could anyone do such a thing, no matter what the reason,
knowing the devastation it would cause? I am numb...*

*

A dog's sharp bark punctured Madeline's sleep.
Shaking herself clear of the sad dream, she looked up to see
the bus rounding the corner. She picked up her bag and
started walking to the corner to meet the bus. The yippy
little dog followed her.

"Don't let that dog in!" exclaimed Sam.

It was too late. The chocolate terrier raced down the
aisle of the bus, causing shrieks and laugher as it skidded to
a halt at the restroom door in the back of the bus.

"Somebody catch that thing," Sam ordered, "before it
demolishes my bus."

Kathy knelt in front of the frightened puppy and spoke
softly to it. She waited until its eyes settled on her and then
slowly placed her hand on the floor in front of it. Then she
let the dog sniff her hand while she continued speaking in
her sing-song voice. As the dog calmed down, she
gradually moved her other hand around until she could
safely pick him up.

"There you go," she said as she deposited him on the
grass on the opposite side of the bus door. "Go home, little
one."

"Thank you, Kathy," Emily said as she climbed into the
bus behind her. "Where did you learn such clever dog-
handling tricks?"

"Sons," she laughingly replied.

Kathy made her way back to her seat next to Terry.
Yes, her sons had taught her much over the years and she
had just been thinking about one of them less than an hour

before. Fort Wilkins had spread before her in a neat rectangle covered by a sharp blue sky. The costumed interpreters had just given Kathy a sense of life in this often adverse environment. It seemed that it was the lot of soldiers of every age to endure hardship and loneliness, along with their meager lifestyle. The only thing they appeared to own in large measure was their loyalty to their country.

As she examined the items displayed in the glass case, she had spotted a collection of old toy soldiers and a memory had flared like a lantern catching to the match.

My Little Gossip

Kathy unscrewed the top of the thermos and filled her cup with the dark roasted brew. Waiting for the coffee to cool slightly, she leaned back and tucked the blanket more securely around her sleeping baby daughter.

"Mom. Mom!" One 'Mom' was never enough for Bobby. He leaned his elbows on the open window. "Guess what? Kenny got in trouble at latch key again—he climbed up on a shelf to get a snack. Everyone knows you're not supposed to do that."

"Don't put your fingers on the mirror, Sweetie. You'll get fingerprints all over it." At eight years old, her middle child was enormously curious about everything, and lately seemed to favor learning through his sense of touch. "So, what happened to Kenny?"

"Miss Schutze called his mother. Then he really got into trouble," he reported.

"I know you are outside, but lower your voice so you don't wake your sister. How did Kenny get into more trouble?"

"He told Miss Schutze a big story. He said that he climbed up on the shelf because he wasn't thinking because

108

he was tired. He told her that he had stayed too late at the fall county fair 'cause his horse was winning a blue ribbon."

"Horse? Kenny doesn't have a horse—he lives in town."

"I know. That's why he's in so much trouble," Bobby concluded before dashing off to the sidelines of the football field to watch his older brother play.

Kathy took a sip of her coffee. Her sons were so different; Joey tackled every activity with a serious intent to succeed and achieve, while Bobby was strictly hit or miss with his success record. She doubted that the three-year age gap between the two accounted for this difference. Bobby was her little gossip and what Joey didn't tell her about school, Bobby filled in, complete with details.

She picked up the toy soldier Bobby had left tucked into the mirror, its plastic gun pointing at the football field. Her son was simply obsessed with his soldiers and she found them stationed everywhere, always propped up in some guarding position. Bobby felt the same protectiveness towards his baby sister, sometimes to a fault; she would face a challenge as she got older.

Kathy smiled to herself. Sounds like Miss Schutze has her challenges, too, she mused. Miss Schutze was in her third year of teaching at the Lutheran school Kathy's sons attended.

"Mom. Mom! Stephanie's here. She came to see her boyfriend play." Bobby had returned with more news.

"Boyfriend? She's in the third grade, for goodness' sake."

"I know. She's in my class. Miss Schutze says she doesn't want to hear about any girls in the third grade having boyfriends." Bobby pulled a soldier out of his pocket and aimed it at the rearview mirror. He knew never to point his toy soldiers at anything alive.

"I think Miss Schutze wants a boyfriend," he confided. "Stephanie told her she would never get a boyfriend if she didn't wear two earrings that matched."

"What did Miss Schutze say to that?" Kathy inquired curiously.

"She didn't say anything about that—she just took Stephanie's jangle bracelet away and told her she could have it back after school."

"Does Stephanie's boyfriend like her?" his mother asked.

"No," Bobby replied soberly. "He told everybody— except Stephanie—that he hates her. Miss Schutze said 'hate' is not a word we should use."

Bobby turned away and dove into the leaves piled near the curb, thrusting them into the wind. Kathy turned her attention to the play on the field. Joey seemed to be getting lots of play time today. His coach sometimes struggled between his desire to win and balancing the development of his players.

"Mom. Mom!" Bobby stood breathlessly at the car window.

"Bobby, you are going to wake the baby. Calm down."

"But Mom, I just thought of something. Guess what? Kenny told Miss Schutze that he swallowed a crayon. But he really didn't—he stuck it in his ear to fool her. Miss Schutze made the whole class listen to the story about the boy who cried wolf. Kenny had to go to the principal's office."

Kathy grinned. "Do you have all your soldiers rounded up? You had better take roll call, the game is almost over. " She hoped he would outgrow his fascination with the soldiers before he got too much older. They say childhood is a rehearsal for adulthood and she couldn't bear to think of her son as a real soldier someday.

110

*

'Someday' had seemed so far away at the time but now she knew twenty-eight years could pass as swiftly as the water flowed over the many waterfalls she had seen on this trip.

She smoothed the canvas into the hoop and consulted the small picture in her lap. This pattern called for three shades of gold embroidery thread and she carefully pulled the ends loose from the thread holder. She had time to complete one more before they stopped for supper.

"What are you making, Kathy?" Terry inquired.

"I'm making a cover for a jar of home-made jelly. These are designs to cross-stitch chrismons."

Terry looked at her in bewilderment. "What in the world are chrismons?"

Kathy chuckled. "They are Christian symbols that are often used as Christmas decorations. I'm using the designs to make the jar covers because I want to give jars of preserves as favors to my guests at the Advent Tea this Christmas."

"Okay. What's an Advent Tea?"

"It's a tradition at my church where right after Thanksgiving, before everyone gets too caught up in the chores of the holiday, we take time to kick off the season quietly. They set up tables in the church basement and women volunteer to host a table. They invite family, friends or even strangers to their tables, which they decorate however they want. We enjoy refreshments and a little social time. Then we all go upstairs to the church and we have a candlelight service of readings and music, all given by the women of the church. It's the only church service of the year that is just for women. We get the season off to a reflective start together."

"That sounds beautiful," Terry whispered.

"I love hosting a table and giving my guests a little treat to take home. That thimbleberry jam I bought in Copper Harbor will be a delicious treat this year."

"Have you always been a church member, Kathy?" Terry was intrigued by how people arrived at their various beliefs and was not the least bit shy about satisfying her curiosity.

"Oh, I went to Sunday school as a child but fell away during my teen years. I didn't think about it again until I was married and pregnant with my first child. My husband and I thought it was important to give our child some kind of spiritual foundation so we started looking for a church to call home."

"That can be a long search," Terry commented. She had drifted in and out of various churches her whole life, never really settling into one.

"It did take us a while but we found our home church in an interesting way. We had skipped around to the churches in our area but hadn't found one that seemed right for us. One Sunday morning we were eating breakfast at a family restaurant and my husband dropped his napkin under the booth. When he reached down to pick it up, he found an offering envelope for a nearby church on the floor. He suggested we drop it off at the church on our way home.

The service was just starting when we got there and the ushers welcomed us and offered to find us a place to sit. We hadn't intended to stay but the usher had already handed us a service folder and was leading us to a pew. So we stayed.

The first thing I noticed was an insert in the folder that had some information about upcoming events, and then it had a joke. It was a question about how many people of various denominations it took to change a light bulb. We were in a Lutheran church and the answer for Lutherans was none—Lutherans don't believe in change.

We liked that the church had a sense of humor about itself and that it was friendly and we both were captivated by the message we heard. Then we discovered that it also sponsored its own school and my husband had heard that Lutheran schools offered a great education. We've been members ever since."

Terry sat back in her seat. "That is interesting. It must be nice to be part of a church family," she said wistfully. "Sometimes communities such as churches are more like family than a family."

"That is so true, Terry. It becomes a built-in support system that you can count on whenever you need it. And the kids did get a good education."

"It's always good to have a shot at going to college directly. My brother joined the Army so he could get his college education funded that way. He's a medical technician now."

"It just delayed time with the Army for my son," Kathy responded. "Bobby graduated from college with a major in journalism and then he promptly volunteered when his employer needed foreign correspondents to be embedded with the troops in Afghanistan. I certainly leaned on my friends at church to see me through that assignment."

"Oh, he is safe, isn't he?" Terry asked anxiously. She constantly worried about her brother who insisted upon re-enlisting time after time.

"Yes, he's home now and a girl has caught his eye, so maybe he'll be less inclined to volunteer for the next dangerous assignment."

*

"I'm glad we are only a half hour from the motel—that was a great buffet and I am stuffed," Emily commented to Sam. "The whitefish up here is just spectacular."

"Amen to that. Now, if you can just get these women to dawdle a tad faster I can put this bus into gear."

But Emily had already headed down the aisle to assist in getting her guests settled in their seats. She paused when she noticed the empty seat next to Leslie.

"Where's Aunt Helen? I know I saw her get on the bus."

Leslie waved vaguely toward the rear of the bus. "She is sitting between the Nelson sisters. They've had an unusually contentious day."

"Oh, dear, I haven't been around them much today. I can do that, so she can be with you," Emily replied.

"Why don't you sit with me instead? She enjoys mediating delicate situations and I am glad she has regained her energy."

Emily dropped into the empty seat. "She certainly has become special to many of the women on this trip."

"That's her way," Leslie replied. "She's one of those rare individuals who can find just the right place to be in a troubled conversation or an awkward situation. We were in one of those family-run tourist shops today and there was a baby wailing away in the arms of the father trying to ring up sales. Aunt Helen simply took the child and worked her magic. The child was soon asleep."

Darkness wrapped the bus in a quiet cocoon of low chatter as they followed the curvy highway back to their motel in L'Anse.

Mourning Dove

A wailing siren pierced the thin layer of sleep cradling Jackie's consciousness. The sudden silence that followed, accompanied by pulses of red light against the blackness of the motel wall, brought her fully awake. She saw that Evelyn was already pulling the window curtain aside.

"Oh, no, it has stopped in front of one of our rooms," she whispered softly to Jackie. The tour group had been assigned the entire row of first-floor rooms on the northern side of the motel complex.

They each grabbed a wrap to ward off the morning chill and stepped outside to join the quickly gathering group of travelers. Terry stood clutching a teddy bear that was dressed in army fatigues. Her plaid flannel shirt tails nearly touched the ground below her bare feet. Madeline stood guard between the rescue squad and the small band of onlookers.

"Who is it?" Jackie asked Sam.

"Aunt Helen. Leslie called 911 and then called Emily and told her that Helen seemed to be having a stroke of some kind. She said Helen had tried to get up but her right leg and arm felt numb. Leslie woke up to the sound of her falling to the floor."

The women stood in respectful silence as the medical responders lifted Helen into the rescue vehicle and helped Leslie in after her.

Emily joined the circle of women. "She's in good hands, ladies, and she was responsive to their questions. Leslie has my cell phone number and will call me as soon as she has more information," Emily informed them calmly. "Let's delay our departure by an hour so we aren't too rushed this morning. I think it will help us all to get an update on Helen before we leave here."

*

Leslie stared at the clear liquid being infused into the IV drip. The paramedic had reassured her that because she had recognized the stroke symptoms immediately, the clot-busting drug had been administered in time to be most effective. Helen's eyes were closed but Leslie knew that she was conscious, conserving her energy for the physical fight ahead. She leaned back against the cold metal of the rescue squad wall and let the raw emotion of the moment carry her back to the last time she remembered feeling so vulnerable.

*

The thunderclap broke over Leslie's head as she dashed from the alley into the back door of Timeless Treasures, her parents' antique shop. Pushing the door shut against the driving rain, she shook the umbrella free of excess water and dropped it into the nearby umbrella stand. The old stand could hold five umbrellas in its brass rings, which were designed to allow each to unfurl into a small circle of swirls so it would dry more quickly. Brass leaves caught the drips at the bottom of the stand as tiny brass hummingbirds circled the top.

It was but one of the thousands of antiques in the warehouse. Her parents had purchased an old Boston building and had taken a great deal of pride in restoring it as a repository for their extensive inventory. Her mother's knack for interior design was evident everywhere—from the store lobby that faced the busy street to the storage attics on the third floor.

Leslie poked her head into her dad's office and saw Arnold sitting at the old roll-top desk, carefully sorting papers into neat piles. Arnold had overseen the accounting side of the business since the day it had opened, so it wasn't a shock to see him sitting there instead of her dad.

"I'm here, Arnold," she announced. "I'm going upstairs for a while."

Arnold nodded and continued to sort the stack in front of him. He was a patient man. He knew Leslie would talk when she was ready. He also knew how she would struggle with the decision before her. Nearly two months had passed since her parents had been found in the wreckage of a small aircraft in Kenya. As their sole beneficiary Leslie would soon have to make a decision as to whether she would take over the running of the business or sell it.

The warehouse stood three stories high. The first floor showcased the most frequently requested items, while the second and third floors were divided into large rooms, each displaying pieces that picked up on a cultural theme. Her mother had created a focal point in each room to show how the pieces could work together to create a certain ambience, a unique atmosphere. The remaining collection of related items surrounded the individual displays.

Leslie's favorite was the Asian room on the third floor. She paused in the doorway to see what had been newly acquired since her last visit. The room had always been her personal retreat. Its focal point was a cozy seating arrangement under the tall windows. The inviting sanctuary was anchored by a fabulous oriental rug on the dark wooden floor and lit by the mellow glow from one of the many vintage lanterns in the collection. A low table set with a Japanese tea service usually graced the center of the setting. The little alcove included Leslie's reading chair, an item that somehow always managed to remain unsold. During her childhood she had spent many hours curled up in that chair, reading her way to world-wide adventures that animated and made special the objects around her.

Looking around the room now, she quickly found the most interesting piece. She walked over to the neatly typed description and read *Chinese Kia King Coromandel screen, 18th century*. It was a twelve-panel folding screen intricately decorated with court scenes on the front panels and rural scenes on the reverse side. Leslie kneeled down to examine it more closely—now this was a piece she and her childhood friend Adam would have found quite fascinating and useful.

Adam's father owned a funeral parlor. Playing hide and seek was their favorite game, as the possibilities for hiding were endless; whether they played among the "dead people" at Adam's father's place or among the "dead things," as he called them, at the antique warehouse. Of course, they were never allowed to play at the funeral home when viewings were occurring and there were plenty of off-limits places in the warehouse, too. Nevertheless, they had found many hours of entertainment between the two settings, with the challenge of escaping parental trouble adding spice to the game.

Emily dropped wearily into the chair under the window and stared at the rain drizzling mournfully down the old glass panes. What was she going to do now? Suddenly, the tears that would not come during the funerals of her parents were flowing as steadily as the rain outside.

"I thought I'd find you here. May I come in?" Aunt Helen inquired quietly from the doorway. Leslie turned from the window and simply nodded.

Helen made her way carefully around the merchandise to the window where Leslie sat and leaned against the sill to look outside.

"I see the mourning doves have taken over the window box again—there's an egg among the petunias."

"I hadn't noticed," Leslie mumbled, doves being the furthest thing from her mind at the moment.

"This is even harder for you than Steve's death," Helen stated quietly. "Do you know why?" Helen dragged over a tapestry-covered foot rest and sat down, ready to listen.

Leslie leaned back against the wing of the old chair, pulled up her knees, and folded her arms around them. The self-hug had become a habit in the two years since Steve's death.

She lifted her tear-streaked face and looked at Helen. "You are very perceptive and I won't argue. I think I know why—I think I feel guilty that I mourn Steve more than I do my parents."

Helen brushed a strand of iron-gray hair back into the French braid that lay against her neck and waited for Leslie to continue.

"I grew up with frequent separations from my parents while they went on their travels to find new treasures for their business, and I went to boarding school as soon as I was old enough. I was never separated from Steve once we were married, but we only had a year together. Now I think I am angry that I seem to have had so little time with both my parents and

Steve. But I feel guilty that I don't sense the loss of them like I think I should."

"They are different kinds of losses, Leslie. Steve was the loss of your future with him. Losing your parents means losing the opportunity to continue building a past with them."

Leslie rested her head in her hands and thought about Helen's words. "I suppose that's why I am so torn about whether to keep the business or sell it," she finally said. "Maybe I believe that if I keep the business they loved so much I will somehow keep their love for me alive."

Helen stood up and looked out the rain-streaked window at the heavy clouds clinging to the sky line. The mourning doves were cooing gently under the eaves.

"Do you love the business, Leslie?"

"I don't know," she answered honestly. "I am afraid I don't have the skills and business knowledge I need. I never wanted to go on their exploration trips with them or to learn how to negotiate prices—or even identify value in the things they found. It would be a huge challenge."

"You are looking at the holes in the Swiss cheese, my dear. Look at the substance. Do you love the business?"

A rumble of thunder followed by a quick flash of lightening startled the doves in the window box. They took off screaming into the rain.

"I want to be like those doves, Aunt Helen. I want to go screaming into the rain."

"The doves will be back. They have that egg to nurture."

Leslie stood up and looked around the room that had been her refuge over the years. It was still crammed with many interesting objects that would delight a future buyer, yet the space seemed empty to her now.

"No, I don't love the business, Aunt Helen. My parents loved the business. I need to build my own nest and fill it with an egg to nurture."

*

The paramedic's gentle tap on her shoulder brought Leslie back to the present. They had arrived at the hospital. She was relieved to see Aunt Helen's eyes open and alert.

Open Mic

The dining room went silent at the sound of Emily's cell phone ringing. Coffee cups were placed silently in saucers and heads craned forward as they waited expectantly for the news.

"Thank you, Leslie," they heard her say. "I am sure you are very relieved." She nodded several times while hurriedly jotting notes on a paper napkin. "Okay, I'll be in touch. Thank you."

Emily stood up and looked at the concerned faces before her.

"Helen is going to be fine. The doctors believe she suffered a mild transient stroke but expect her to make a full recovery without permanent damage. The drug the paramedics gave her was very effective in breaking up the clot that threatened her life. They are going to keep her in the hospital for 48 hours for monitoring and then they will fly back home to Boston. Both Leslie and Helen express their thanks and gratitude for your thoughts and prayers and wish you a happy journey for the remainder of the trip."

Emily turned to Sam and consulted with him briefly.

"Sam says the bus is loaded and we will leave in approximately fifteen minutes. We will drive to Crystal

Falls and enjoy a box lunch at a lovely park there. Then we'll drive on to Iron Mountain where we will have the opportunity to tour the Iron Mountain Iron Mine and Museum this afternoon. Tonight, of course, we will end our tour with a fabulous dinner with a family at their farm house. I promise you—that will be a wonderful treat for us all," she concluded with a warm smile.

"On board, ladies," Sam ordered as he headed to the door. "No dawdling—this means you, Terry. There's a beautiful day waiting for us."

Yes, thought Emily, a beautiful day indeed. But the cloud of concern that had come with the day had left its shadow and Emily felt she needed to restore the brightness to this last full day together on the Dream Catcher Tour. She didn't think playing bingo or watching a video was going to be enough of a distraction from the dramatic events of the morning. She knew the women would see the two empty seats and immediately be reminded of how quickly lives can change. Her grandmother's advice came to mind.

"Emily, dolly, you've got to look a problem in the face if you ever want to see the back of its head." Yes, that advice made sense to her this morning. Now, how did she apply it?

"Sam, where's the wireless microphone?" Emily asked as she fished around in the box behind the driver's seat.

"Why? What are you planning?" Sam responded with his own question.

"I'm going to host an open mic session," she said as she pulled the microphone from the box. "How does this thing work?"

Sam rolled his eyes and concentrated on his driving.

"Ladies, may I have your attention, please?" Emily walked slowly down the aisle testing the volume on the wireless microphone.

"I've noticed throughout this tour that many of you picked up regional cookbooks as we traveled throughout the Upper Peninsula. My mother collected recipes too, and even though she didn't make very many of them, she said she enjoyed just reading them. How many of you buy cookbooks just to read?"

Emily was not surprised to see many hands go up. "That's what I thought. Why do we do that?" Emily paused and looked expectantly at the women.

"It's the stories," said Betty. "Our favorite recipes always have a story behind them."

"That's true. Who else has a thought about why we like reading recipes?" Emily looked around and handed the microphone to Marianne, who was smiling shyly at her.

"And because food is such a big part of our socialization. The recipes tell us about the culture and history of different people. It's a way of traveling and sharing without even leaving your own home."

Kathy took the mic from Marianne. "It's like eating comfort food to me. I read those recipes and I feel a connection to the woman who made it and I know I'm not alone in the daily battle to keep my family fed and content."

Emily took the microphone and walked further down the aisle. "Would you like to start an impromptu Dream Catcher Tour collection of recipes? If you share a recipe and a story to go with it, I'll write it down and get copies made for whoever would like them. We've got over an hour before our next stop. What do you think?"

"I'd like that," Madeline replied, "and I'll start. Are you ready?"

"Wait until I get my laptop out," Emily laughed.

Madeline took the microphone and walked to the front of the bus. "This is a recipe to keep a troublesome old aunt out of trouble. Naturally, she is my husband's relation and she is the worst cook in our part of the country. After three consecutive Thanksgiving meals where she was responsible for a main dish that turned out to be inedible, someone suggested that we have yearly assignments, where each person brings the same thing every year. We all thought this was a great idea and the old aunt was assigned jello salad. She was disappointed but we told her that it would be special if she could somehow use cranberries or cranberry flavors in it so it would be very special Thanksgiving jello. We figured that since men and children generally don't eat jello with fruit in it, it wouldn't do any harm to the menu. Well, she took this very seriously, and every year she comes up with a different—yet awful—variation of the basic red jello theme. But she feels she is contributing, and the rest of us don't feel guilty for pushing it politely around the salad plate until it melts into a little puddle of fruit. She is providing a yearly conversation piece."

Emily perched her laptop on her knees and looked at Madeline. "I'm ready."

Madeline nodded. "The title is No Trouble Jello and the ingredients are one small package of any red jello and one small package of any other kind of jello. Prepare according to the box directions and let chill until thickened but not set. Add chopped cranberries or strawberries or apples or chopped celery or chopped nuts—anything except miniature marshmallows. Chill until firm and serve topped with whipped topping."

"So, how can she mess up a basic recipe like that?" Lynn asked.

Maddie sighed. "It's the liquid. She thinks water is too plain so she adds something 'with a little kick,' like bourbon. It's classic too-much-of-a-good-thing."

After the laughter died down, Kathy took the microphone.

"I found a cookbook a couple of days ago that described all the different types of aprons church women used to wear when volunteering at a luncheon. There was a basic serving apron, a fancy anniversary apron, a frilly wedding apron…even a catch-all apron that covered from head to toe that was no doubt wrapped around children at spaghetti suppers. It reminded me of the aprons my grandmother sewed. I still have one. It's a green and white gingham checked one with a single pocket and a row of yellow chicks cross-stitched across the wide border of the hem. I love that keepsake."

Terry laughed. "I don't even own one apron, much less more than one!"

Emily smiled to herself as she swiftly captured the stories and recipes the women shared. Talking about food and family had broken the somber spell of the morning and the women would be more than ready for their box lunch treat by noon. She would have to remember to tell them that the salad was made with sensible macaroni and snappy cheese—at least, that was how the caterer had described it.

Underground

"Lynn, maybe they'll let you buy that hard hat and you can wear it while on playground duty. That would really protect you when a dodgeball game gets wild," Maggie said.

"Maybe I'll just wear this bright yellow rain jacket instead so they can see me better," Lynn retorted.

Amy adjusted the strap of the helmet and looked at her friends. "We should all buy the hard hats and then wear them when we go on our annual shopping trip the day after Thanksgiving. That will help us get through the crowds."

"And we'll be able to spot each other more easily when we get separated," Maddie contributed.

The four women joined the others to get on the train for the underground tour of the Iron Mountain Iron Mine. They had been told to wear sweaters or jackets since the wet, cool climate underground was a constant 43 degrees year-round. While many of their group had opted out of the mine tour, the teachers were looking forward to the experience. The fascinating rock and gift shop would certainly entertain the others during the half-hour tour.

"Now, Maddie, don't get all wrapped up in this and spend the rest of the day writing up lesson plans," Amy teased. "We only have tonight left and I'm sure you don't want to miss dinner on the farm."

"Don't worry. I've got that out of my system for this trip," Madeline replied. "But I may take a few notes."

The women got on board the train and settled back for the trip through the 2,600 feet of the East Vulcan Mine. The cold, damp air immediately surrounded them as they descended into the dimly lit shaft.

"We've added extra lighting so that you can see the formations but later we will turn off the lights so that you can see the candle illumination the miners would have worked under," the guide began. "This is the very same railway system that the miners used to get to their workplace each day."

Above ground, Ruth and Betty were exploring the large gift shop along with other members of their group who had not taken the underground mine tour. "Betty, look at these rock collections. This might be a souvenir idea for my grandson—he's just at that age when it's fun to collect things and stash them away in old cigar boxes. He likes to trade with his friends, too, and this would be something different from the usual sports cards."

Ruth examined the boxes of rocks. "There certainly are a lot of choices. Are you thinking of something more educational or just shiny and bright?"

"He's only seven. I think the simpler the better. He loves colorful things. How about this set that has a lot of quartz in it?"

"I'm sure he'll be thrilled with whatever you bring him. Now, what about his sister? Do you have something for her yet?"

"No, but this place has a lot of copper jewelry so I'll check that section out next. It will be easy to find a gift for her."

Emily helped Jackie negotiate the doorway to step outside and then went over to the picnic table to join Sam.

"We should be in Harris by four o'clock. That will give the ladies plenty of time to get settled in at the Chip-In Island Resort hotel and be ready to leave for the farm dinner by five," Sam said as he looked up from the map he had been studying.

Emily slid onto the bench beside him. "What about the directions to the Zettlemans' farm? I'm really looking forward to the dinner and entertainment tonight."

"No problem. The directions are straightforward. I've never attended an 'agra-entertainment' before. It should be fun."

"It's a great way to end the tour. The Zettlemans love entertaining groups and their cook-outs are very popular with the tour groups. The farmers struggle so much in this economy, and I think the creative ideas they've come up with to keep their farms going are admirable."

Sam leaned back to see how many more members of the group had drifted out of the gift shop to enjoy the fresh air and be lulled by the breeze rifling through the pines. "Summer is short up here. I don't see how it can help them that much."

Emily smiled. "I said they were creative. Mr. Zettleman creates a corn maze in his fields in the fall and the entertainment changes to haunted hayrides. He bought a sleigh for winter moonlight rides and in spring he offers a maple sugaring tour. He's very popular with youth groups and school field trips, so he has built year-round support into his business."

"It looks like the mine tour is over," Sam said, nodding to the group of people filing out of the mine entrance. "Let's get them on the bus."

Farm Fair

S am came to a complete stop at the intersection although there were no stop signs in view. The corn in the fields had grown to a height that made it difficult to see cross traffic. But the country roads were deserted, so he made the sharp turn and started looking for the mail box identifying the Zettleman farm.

"The driveway is just past that row of newspaper holders," Emily said.

The farm came into view as Sam followed the gravel driveway flanked by corn fields. He spotted the hand-lettered Bus Parking sign and pulled into a space carved in the field.

"Welcome to the Zettleman farm," Pete Zettleman proclaimed in a deep baritone voice. He was a middle-aged man of average height, with a balding head now exposed as he held his cap in his hand. A sandy mustache shot with gray lined his upper lip. Clean but well-worn bib overalls covered a faded blue denim shirt with sleeves folded back over his deeply tanned arms.

"On behalf of my family and farm hands, we extend to you our enthusiastic hospitality and entertainment this beautiful evening. Zach and Tyler are standing by to assist you."

Peter Zettleman stepped back off the bus where Zach was waiting to help anyone who needed support in stepping down to the gravel driveway. Tyler, who obviously had no need of it, leaned on a striking hand-carved walking stick and waited to lead the group through the farm gate to the house. The young men appeared to be brothers, with identical friendly smiles.

Marilyn turned on her camera and walked to a fence surrounding a mud hole while her companions exited the bus. A huge hog lounged near one edge, its feet in murky water and head curled back facing the evening sun. The pungent odor of farm animals assailed her senses. Lifting the viewfinder to frame the tranquil scene, she carefully composed the shot and pressed the shutter.

"Don't tell me you're going to use that in one of your decorating schemes," laughed Jody.

"No, and I don't think I'll worry if I forget this view, either," Marilyn replied. "I just want to document it for my trip scrapbook."

Jody sighed with envy. She loved the idea of having a trip scrapbook or even a photo album of one of the most enjoyable and relaxing trips of her life but she just wasn't a crafty person.

"How about if you make two copies and sell one to me?" Jody joked. "We have seen basically the same things."

Marilyn tucked the camera in her pocket as they walked back to the group. "You took pictures, too—aren't you going to do something with them?"

Jody nodded. "I expect I'll do my usual thing—keep them in the envelopes they came in from the processor and pass them around to those of my family and friends who I think can tolerate seeing them."

Tyler led the forty-five women and Sam and Emily through the gate and began his introductory speech.

"The Zettleman farm was established in 1919 and started out with a small house, a barn, and a chicken coop. As you can see, we've grown some since then. Today we grow mostly corn and we raise a few head of market cattle and hogs. We do a little maple sugaring in the spring, too, but our favorite means of support is hosting groups such as yours for lovely little entertainments."

He led them to a huge barn with long tables set up down the center. The tables were covered in red-and-white checkered plastic tablecloths with baskets of silverware and napkins spaced along their length, punctuated occasionally by a glass canning jar filled with colorful summer flowers.

Along one wall of the barn a line of stalls had been converted to craft booths. A hand-painted wooden sign hanging above the row read 'Holiday Blend' and each stall displayed items related to a specific season or seasonal theme beginning with summer and ending with winter. Small street signs identified each stall with names of native trees: Oak Drive, Cedar Lane, Pine Way, Birch Court, and Poplar Street.

"Welcome to our home," Florence Zettleman said. She adjusted the soft straw hat that had slipped over eyes as brown as the cows she tended. Wrinkles radiated from her wide, warm smile. "We hope you enjoy your evening with us. Pete is ready to begin grilling, so feel free to browse around for a few minutes. All the crafts and gift baskets are handmade by friends and neighbors in our area. If you want to buy something, simply take the item to Hannah, who will be at the table under the sign and she will check you out."

"Do you take credit cards?" called a voice from the back of the group.

Florence nodded and said, "Yes, whatever is convenient for you. Are there any other questions?" She paused and looked around. The women were already moving towards the craft stalls.

"When the meat is ready, you will hear the cow bell ring three times. Please go to the table that will be serving the entrée you prefer." The first table in each line sported a picture of a cow, chicken, or pig.

Just outside the barn there was an above-ground fire pit with a galvanized steel cover, in which a whole pig was being roasted. Several large grills on either side of the pit were being tended by the farm hands as hamburgers and ribs released their delicious fragrance on one side and barbecued chicken cooked on the other. A large tripod stood over another charcoal fire with a giant pot of boiling water hanging from its center hook. Two more farm hands were shucking corn from the fields and tossing it into waiting water pots nearby.

Several young girls carried covered dishes from the house to a warming/cooling station set up just inside the front barn wall. A line of outlets paraded along a strip above the tables. Several warming plates crowded together on one table in wait for the colorful covered bowls coming from the kitchen ovens. A few feet away a second table, custom built, had been filled with ice to chill potato salad, coleslaw and a variety of other salads. A bread rack with covered rolls stood next to a bright red 1950s stove under a small window. Several pie safes were packed with an assortment of pies that would be served with ice cream for dessert.

Jackie leaned her cane against the display bench and picked up the scarecrow to examine it more closely.

"This is just adorable!" she said to Evelyn. "I love the way she's dressed—the hat and matching purse are so clever."

Evelyn set down the magic pumpkin coach she was holding and joined Jackie. "She's ready to shop, all right.

This whole place is so cleverly done," she commented as she looked around. A door in the back wall of the barn led to another large room that was set up for the entertainment to be held later. An oversized dream catcher hung above the door with a tableau of clay characters from Charlotte's Web staged on the ledge on top of the door. A silk spider web woven into the corner arch sparkled with glitter, giving it a fresh, just rained-on appearance.

The sound of the cow bell echoed throughout the barn.

"Oh, dear, decision time," Jackie said as she reached for her cane. "I can't decide between the ribs or the chicken."

"No problem here—that roasted pig smells heavenly!"

"Lemonade or iced tea?" asked the blond teenager in jean shorts and a halter top, as she moved down the long table with a pitcher in each hand. "We have coffee and soft drinks, too."

Ruth held her glass out. "My grandmother made the best lemonade for us when we were kids. She called it her white lightning and she served it with graham crackers dripping in frosting."

Linda looked at the steaming platter of corn on the cob in front of her. "Oh, yes, this place is bringing out all my favorite food memories. I remember those hot summer nights in northern Wisconsin when it was too hot to cook. My mother would boil up some corn on the cob and serve it with tomatoes freshly picked from her garden. Such a simple supper, but it sure hit the spot—especially when it was topped off by a trip to the ice cream parlor afterwards."

"Yes," Ruth laughed. "But back then our stomachs could handle anything."

Emily looked around at the tables filled with the people she had come to know over the last ten days. The sound of happy chatter surrounded her, setting up a harmony in her heart that she had not felt in a long time. Like the intertwining strands of the dream catcher above the door, she had acquired a few more strings around her heart that helped secure her confidence in her place in this world at this time of her life. Perhaps life wasn't linear after all, she thought, with a beginning, middle, and end. Maybe it was more like a spiral, with each day and every experience flowing together to form intersections where points of strength were built. Life traveled along the lines of the day, securing hopes and dreams, while nightmares slowly drained through the empty spaces of mistakes and regrets.

"You undersold this place, Emily," Sam remarked as he slid into the folding chair next to her. "The food is fabulous, just fabulous."

Emily shifted her chair back and turned to him. "That's why I schedule it for the last night of the tour. I see you've made yourself right at home," she observed, noting his rolled-up sleeves and the tie peeking from his front shirt pocket.

Sam grinned. "I'm not driving the bus right now."

"Well, you may feel like you are when you see the entertainment," she replied mysteriously.

"Then I'm going to need another piece of this apple pie."

The cow bell rang again. "May I have your attention, please?" Mr. Zettleman requested. He stood on a bale of hay and waited for the women to quiet down.

"We are ready to begin the entertainment for the evening. If you would, please move into the back room of the barn, find a comfortable spot to sit down, and we'll get started."

The women spilled through the door to a large room with a wooden stage centered against the back wall. Tiny white lights twinkled across the top frame while decorative bird houses line the front edge shelf just below the stage itself. Bales of hay, arranged in rows and columns with an aisle between, were angled to face the stage. A colorful, thick rag rug covered each bale of hay to provide comfortable seating. Several large patterned quilts hung from the rafters as backdrops for the stage. Large fans along the side walls kept the warm summer air moving freely.

A full set of drums took center stage with the name of the group, The Tourist Trappers, emblazoned across the face of the kick drum. Each 's' in the band's logo was a dollar sign. Microphones hung from the rafters and huge speakers flanked the stage.

Terry, Lois and Betty found seats up front, with the Fearsome 4Sum taking up residence right behind them.

"Do you think it's going to be too loud this close to those speakers?" Lois asked.

"The speakers are probably more for show than anything else. We'll just cover our ears if they blast us and they'll get the idea."

Madeline leaned forward. "I'll just tell them to pipe down if it's uncomfortable."

Her friends laughed. "You go, girl!" Lynn encouraged.

Pete Zettleman walked out on the stage, microphone in hand. He tapped it lightly to verify the sound level. Spotlights came on as the lights in the barn dimmed, revealing electric red hurricane lamps hung strategically from the wooden ceiling beams to create a cozy, warm ambience.

"Our performers tonight are musicians from the Escanaba Area High School. Music education has long been a part of the curriculum in Escanaba and our concert and marching bands provide great opportunities for the students in this area. The Tourist Trappers band originally started with my sons but as they grew up and left home to pursue opportunities elsewhere, I had to find replacements. My brother, Harold, has taught music at the school for many years and he keeps me supplied with great young talent. Don't let their youth and fancy equipment unsettle you—they are here to amuse and charm you to no end. Enjoy!"

He set the microphone in the stand and walked to the drum kit, where he settled in among the tom toms and cymbals. A tall, lanky teenager walked onto the stage, picked up his bass, and sat on the tall stool next to the drums. Two more young men, one with a guitar and the other with a banjo, came from the wings to take their positions. Finally, a lovely young lady with strawberry blond curls tumbling to her waist took center stage, with violin and bow in hand. The teenagers were dressed in blue jeans and t-shirts with beads that sparkled under the stage lights.

"Hello, everyone," she spoke into the microphone. "My name is Ashley and I'd like to introduce Josh on the guitar, Jacob on the banjo, and my brother Chris on the bass." The boys nodded in acknowledgement.

They all took up their instruments and a soft strumming began, accompanied by a rhythmic beat on the drums. The guitar and banjo picked out a refrain as Ashley lifted her violin to her chin and began a lively melody. Tempo and volume increased until the barn vibrated with musical energy.

"Wow," Linda whispered to Barb. "They are talented."

The applause faded as the spotlight focused on Jacob. A haunting, provocative tune flowed from his nimble fingers; the sound from the banjo was as unexpected as it was beautiful.

Josh and Chris teamed for a duet, with drum support from Pete Zettleman. The group performed a couple more group numbers and then Ashley stepped forward once more.

"I bet you thought you were going to get hard rock when you saw us," she grinned. When the laughter subsided, she continued.

"The next part of our program is interactive," she announced. "How many of you once rode a big ol' yellow bus to school every day?"

Many hands went up.

"I thought so. Now, let me guess—you did your homework during the long rides home, right?"

The women chuckled and shook their heads.

"Hmm, right about that, too. Let's see if I can go three for three. I'm betting you sang silly songs and really annoyed your bus driver."

The laughter was even louder now. Sam spoke up. "They still annoy the bus driver."

"Sam!" Emily whispered loudly, poking him in the ribs.

Ashley waited until it was quiet once more. "Let's resurrect some of those old favorites tonight. If you would stand up, please, and lift up the rug on your seat, you will find a sing-along sheet underneath."

The women looked at each other warily but complied.

"Okay, let's begin. Someone call out a title."

Terry stood up. "Let's do 'This Old Man', dedicated to our bus driver, Sam."

"The band will play it through once and then we'll begin," Ashley directed. "Mr. Zettleman loves the knick-knack-paddy-whack part, so give him his due."

A half hour later, they had, among other things, seen the bear go over the mountain, lamented the hole in the bucket, and remembered the view from on top of spaghetti.

"You ladies make a great choir! Thank you for your enthusiastic participation. I'll share a little secret with you—the bus songs haven't changed over the years," Ashley confided. "We are going to end tonight with one I hope never changes. We will sing it in a round, after the band sings it through once. Then those sitting on the left side of the aisle will start and I will cue those on the right side when to begin their part of the round. Keep singing until I give you the signal to stop. Ready?"

Mr. Zettleman and the boys joined Ashley along the front of the stage. He lifted the pitch pipe to his lips and softly blew the starting note.

Make new friends, but keep the old...one is silver and the other gold...Make new friends, but keep the old...one is silver and the other gold...

Pathways Home

The morning sky dawned overcast, with humidity noticeably building. It was good weather for traveling home, Emily thought, as she stood in the parking lot waiting for the women to sort through the packages Sam had stored for them in the cargo bay.

"Carol." said Ivy, "I'm pretty sure that is my package. Remember, I bought that honey up in the Keweenaw?"

"Yes, I remember, but where's my package? I bought stuff there, too," Carol replied. "Didn't we combine it into one shopping bag?"

"As usual, Carol, you are right. And, while I'm at it, I will admit that you were right about taking this trip together. I had such a good time."

"I agree with you wholeheartedly there, Ivy."

Sam silently shook his head. He didn't think he'd see the day those two agreed on anything.

Emily looked up as the second bus pulled up alongside of Sam's.

"Ladies, may I have your attention, please?" Emily moved to stand on the bottom step of the bus so they could all hear her clearly.

"I heard from Leslie this morning and Helen is

140

recovering very well and was very sorry she missed enjoying our last night together. They will be flying back home tomorrow.

"The bus taking the northern route back to the Detroit area is ready to load. Please be sure you have all of your packages on the luggage trolley and Sam will transfer them to the other bus. Your new driver is Ed. Your bags are being loaded now.

I'd like to ask the rest of you to double-check your packages, as well, to make sure your name tag is on each bag and box. We will be departing for Chicago as soon as Sam has everything reloaded. Are there any questions?"

Madeline stepped forward. She handed a large manila envelope with their tip money to Emily and a second one to Sam. "I would like to thank you, Emily and Sam, on behalf of my fellow travelers and myself, for the wonderful experiences we've enjoyed on the Dream Catcher Tour sponsored by Northern Experience Tours. Please accept this token of our appreciation for a job well done."

The women applauded loudly and nodded in vigorous agreement.

"Thank you very much," Emily said humbly. "You have been a terrific group and I am thankful that I had the opportunity to share in your vacation time. My life is richer for knowing you."

Sam pulled his cap from his head and held his arms out. "You were great! Thank you!"

The ladies said their final farewells and started boarding the buses for the long trip home. Souvenirs would serve as physical reminders of this small adventure in their lives for a time, but the friendships formed or renewed, and the fellowship experienced, would last them a lifetime.

*

"Matthew, finish your sandwich. We have to get back on the road," the harried young mother instructed. "I'm almost finished feeding the babies and your dad will be back with Bingo soon."

"Mommy," Matthew asked as he squirmed off the picnic table bench. "Who are all those old ladies getting off that bus? Where are they going?"

The mother looked at the sleek, air-conditioned motor coach and sighed in silent envy. "They aren't old ladies, Matty, they are just older than me. And I don't know where they are going. Drink your juice."

I don't even know where I'm going, she thought despairingly. I can't see beyond the next diaper change today. Glancing at the smiling faces milling around the rest area, she made a promise to herself: Someday, I'm going to get on a bus, too, and just see where it takes me. The impulsive dream fueled her soul like the sudden blast of flame in a hot air balloon. She felt her spirits rise.

Author's
Acknowledgements

This book is dedicated to those women everywhere who assume the daily tasks and responsibilities of their roles to nurture healthy and whole families and communities. The threads of their lives form the incredibly rich fabric of our societies. The characters in this book were inspired by their beauty, strength and spirit. I also dedicate this book to those men who support and cherish the women in their lives.

I would like to acknowledge two of the anchors in my life: my dear husband, who is ever tolerant of my little adventures and grand schemes, and my precious mother, who is an unending source of encouragement and love.

My grateful thanks also go out to family members and friends who provided sharp focus and thoughtful feedback throughout the writing and publishing process. Among them, in alphabetical order: Allison, Beth, Bonnie, Diann, Elizabeth, Faith, Gayle G, Grace, Jessica, Katie, Laura,

Paula Buermele

Linda B, Linda H, Lisa, Marci, Mary, Melissa, Rebecca, Rebekah, Rose, Sharon, Susan, Theresa, Val.

I also thank the William Bonifas Fine Arts Center, Lakenenland Sculptures, and Jilbert's Dairy for permission to use their locales in this novel.

Finally, thank you to the owner and staff at Beaner's Coffee in Canton, Michigan, for always making me feel welcome no matter how long I stayed, and also for trying out their new coffee drinks on me.

About the Author

Paula Buermele is an attentive student in the classroom of life. Look for her wonderful wisdom and insights to appear in future works as she continues to transform life's observations, experiences, and recollections into word art to share with her readers. Paula has had previous work published in *Above The Bridge* magazine.

Paula lives in Canton, Michigan, with her husband, Byron.

Visit her website at: www.thedreamcatchertour.com.

Printed in the United States
81802LV00002B/346

9 781432 703530